"You tell me, Bria," he answered. His eyes held hers, and until that moment she hadn't really understood what it meant to feel as if someone's piercing gaze went all the way to her soul.

She caught her breath. Had he remembered something? Maybe a fragment about their marriage being in trouble?

"There used to be a time when you loved for me to let you feel how much I want you," he said. He shook his head. "Now you get jumpy as hell if I get within ten feet of you and try to put as much distance between us as you possibly can."

She should have known that he would start questioning why she kept sidestepping his advances. "Sam, I…"

He gave her a kiss so tender it brought tears to her eyes. "When we go upstairs to bed, I'm going to hold you until all your worries melt away."

"I don't think…that would be a good idea," she said haltingly.

"I do."

Dear Reader,

This month I'm thrilled to tell you about my new miniseries, The Good, the Bad and the Texan. When the foster care system gave up on them as lost causes, six troubled teenage boys were sent to the Last Chance Ranch and the mentoring of rodeo champion Hank Calvert. Using ranch work and rodeo to help them work through their problems, Hank assisted them in overcoming their troubles with the law to grow up to be good, honest, successful men.

In *His Marriage to Remember,* you'll meet rodeo stock contractor Sam Rafferty and his wife, Brianna. They are one signature away from being divorced when the dissolution of their marriage has to be put on hold when Sam is injured in a rodeo accident. While Sam recuperates, he and Brianna have the opportunity to examine the problems behind their breakup and decide if a second chance at making their marriage work is worth the risk to their hearts.

So please, hang on and enjoy getting to know the men raised at the Last Chance Ranch. Running with these billionaires will be one wild ride.

All the best,

Kathie DeNosky

KATHIE DeNOSKY

HIS MARRIAGE
TO REMEMBER

™ Harlequin®

Desire

Recycling programs
for this product may
not exist in your area.

ISBN-13: 978-0-373-73174-9

HIS MARRIAGE TO REMEMBER

www.Harlequin.com

Printed in U.S.A.

Books by Kathie DeNosky

Harlequin Desire

In Bed with the Opposition #2126
Sex, Lies and the Southern Belle #2132
†*His Marriage to Remember* #2161

Silhouette Desire

Cassie's Cowboy Daddy #1439
Cowboy Boss #1457
A Lawman in Her Stocking #1475
In Bed with the Enemy #1521
Lonetree Ranchers: Brant #1528
Lonetree Ranchers: Morgan #1540
Lonetree Ranchers: Colt #1551
Remembering One Wild Night #1559
Baby at His Convenience #1595
A Rare Sensation #1633
*Engagement Between Enemies #1700
*Reunion of Revenge #1707
*Betrothed for the Baby #1712
The Expectant Executive #1759
Mistress of Fortune #1789
*Bossman Billionaire #1957
*One Night, Two Babies #1966
*The Billionaire's Unexpected Heir #1972
Expecting the Rancher's Heir #2036

Silhouette Books

Home for the Holidays
  "New Year's Baby"

*The Illegitimate Heirs
†The Good, the Bad and the Texan

Other titles by this author
available in ebook format.

KATHIE DeNOSKY

lives in her native southern Illinois on the land her family settled in
1839. She writes highly sensual stories with a generous amount of
humor; her books have appeared on the *USA TODAY* bestseller list
and received numerous awards, including two National Reader's
Choice Awards. Kathie enjoys going to rodeos, traveling to research
settings for her books and listening to country music. Readers may
contact her by emailing kathie@kathiedenosky.com. They can also
visit her website, www.kathiedenosky.com, or find her on Facebook,
www.facebook.com/pages/Kathie-DeNosky-Author/278166445536145.

A special thank-you to Kathie Brush
for letting me bounce ideas off her and
for making some very interesting cups of coffee.

And to my editor, Stacy Boyd. Thanks for everything.
I look forward to working on many more books with you.

Prologue

"Hey, Sam! You want to stop gatherin' daisies over there like some little girl and open that gate?" someone called from the platform behind the chutes.

Cursing himself for letting his mind wander, rodeo-stock contractor Sam Rafferty pulled the gate open to guide the next bull down the channel of steel fence panels into the bucking chutes. He needed to keep his mind on what he was doing and forget about the things in his life he couldn't control. Otherwise, somebody would end up getting hurt.

His younger brother, Nate, came to stand beside him as they both watched a bull rider climb over the side of one of the chutes and onto the broad back of Bumblebee, the biggest, meanest Brahma in Sam's string of bucking bulls. Nate's eyes never left the bull, but Sam could tell his younger brother was gauging his mood and how much he should say.

"Bria going to be here today?" Nate finally asked.

"Yup."

Neither man's gaze wavered from the bull and rider.

"You want to talk about it?"

"Nope." Sam clenched his jaw so hard it wouldn't have surprised him if he ended up with a couple of cracked teeth as he waited for Nate to question him further.

Apparently sensing that he was treading on thin ice, Nate wisely nodded as he sauntered away. "Good talk, Sam."

Beyond telling his brothers that he and his wife were getting a divorce, Sam hadn't talked to anyone about the breakup of his marriage and he wasn't about to start now. Bria had her reasons for wanting out. He sure as hell didn't agree with them, but they were important enough to her to walk away from five years of their being together—three of those years being his wife.

When he got the signal from the chute boss, Sam automatically opened the gate again to guide the next bull into the bucking channel. He realized Bria wanted to get the divorce over with so that she could move on with her life, and even if he didn't agree that ending their marriage was the only answer to their problems, he could respect that. But why did she have to choose this particular weekend to bring the papers by for his signature? She knew this was the one time of year that he and his brothers got together to put on the annual Hank Calvert Memorial Rodeo, honoring the foster father who had taken them in and straightened them out when the system had given up on all of them as lost causes.

Allowing another bull to enter the channel, Sam thought about the man who had taken in six troubled teenage boys and saved them from a life behind bars, or worse yet, an early death. A Champion All-Around Rodeo Cowboy, Hank had ridden in all the rough-stock events and amassed a sizable fortune by the time he retired at the ripe old age of thirty-eight. But instead of spending his winnings on pleasurable pursuits, Hank had started the Last Chance Ranch for troubled boys, because as he had told them time and again, there was no such thing as a lost cause when it came to people. They had the free will to change—to rise above their circumstances and make something better of themselves.

Sam took a deep breath as he thought about the man whose life was cut short way too soon by a massive heart attack. Hank had wisely used ranch work and rodeo to help him and his brothers work through the anger and aggression they felt over the injustices they had suffered in their young lives. He had counseled them, been their mentor and taught them how to be honorable upstanding members of society. He'd encouraged them to stay in school, tutored them when he could, hired someone to do it when it was a subject he knew little about and set up trust funds to help them get a college education. Hank Calvert was directly responsible for making them the men they were today, and they owed the man and his memory more than any of them could ever repay.

That's why it irritated the hell out of him that Bria had insisted that the divorce papers couldn't wait one more day. She knew how important this particular rodeo was to him—to all of them. Why did she have to be so damn eager to be rid of him?

Scanning the crowd in the grandstand, his gaze went to the end of the bleachers, then came back to zero in on the auburn-haired woman climbing the steps to the section of seats reserved for the wives and girlfriends of the riders and rodeo personnel. Even with everything that had happened between them—all the angry accusations and painful disappointments—Bria Stanton-Rafferty still took his breath away, still made his heart beat a little faster whenever he saw her. He had a feeling she probably always would.

When their gazes met, his chest tightened and a knot twisted in his gut. They had reached an impasse and he wasn't going to stand in her way, if ending their marriage was what she really wanted. He cared too much about her to try forcing her to stay in a situation that caused her so much unhappiness.

"Sam!"

"Watch out!"

"Get out of the way, Rafferty!"

The urgent shouts of his brothers and the personnel behind the bucking chutes suddenly broke through his disturbing introspection.

Turning to see why they were so intent on trying to gain his attention, Sam heard the angry bellow at the same time he caught sight of two thousand pounds of pissed-off beef coming at him like a runaway freight train. A big brindle bull had somehow escaped the channel of fence panels and was loose behind the bucking chutes.

With no time to scramble to the top of the fence and nowhere else to go, Sam knew his best hope of avoiding disaster would be to use his hands to try to push off the animal's head and launch himself to the side. Doing just that, he might have been successful had there been more room. But the close quarters in the section of fence panels prevented him from completely avoiding the bull's pass and he felt his head collide with the steel gate at the same time he heard a woman's terrified scream.

Pain shot through his skull with the intensity of a lightning bolt a moment before a dark curtain descended around him. He tried to fight it, tried to keep his eyes open. He needed to reassure Bria, needed to tell her that no matter what happened to him, he wanted nothing but the best for her and for her to be happy. But the throbbing ache in his head was excruciating and closing his eyes, Sam had no choice but to give in and allow himself to sink into the peaceful black abyss of unconsciousness.

One

Standing in the hospital waiting room, Bria wrapped her arms around herself as she tried to chase away the chills. It did no good. In spite of the fact that it was early June in Texas and already extremely warm, she couldn't seem to stop shivering.

Terror like nothing she had ever known had clawed at her insides as she'd helplessly watched the angry bull slam Sam into the fence, then pummel his limp body repeatedly with its large head. Thankfully, the bull didn't have horns and therefore Sam hadn't sustained any puncture wounds, nor had he been stepped on by the massive animal. Nate and Sam's foster brothers had immediately jumped into action and diverted the bull's attention as quickly as they could. But it seemed as if they'd all moved in slow motion and took forever to get the beast away from him so the emergency medical crew could move in and take over.

She drew in a shuddering breath. There was no getting around it, she was responsible for Sam's accident. If she had only waited for another day, another time to bring the divorce papers for him to sign or if he hadn't seen her and been distracted, she wouldn't be standing in the waiting room while he underwent tests to see just how badly he was injured.

But the rodeo was only a two-hour drive from her new home in Dallas and she had wanted to get the papers signed and everything finalized before she started her new job as a marketing consultant for one of the major department stores. If she hadn't run into a traffic jam on the interstate, she would have arrived with plenty of time to get things taken care of and left before the dangerous bull-riding event even started.

Her breath caught on a sob. It didn't matter why she had been running late or that she had wanted to get on with her life. Sam was the one having to pay the price for her impatience.

"Have you heard anything, Bria?" Nate called from somewhere behind her.

Turning around, she watched Nate and his brothers hurrying down the hall toward the waiting-room entrance. Tall and ruggedly handsome, all five men were cowboys from the top of their wide-brimmed Resistol hats to their scuffed Justin boots. All six of the boys Hank Calvert had fostered had grown up to be extremely wealthy men, but to the outward eye, they were down to earth, hardworking cowboys who passed up designer clothing in favor of chambray shirts and jeans. Nate was Sam's only biological sibling, but the other four men they called brothers couldn't have meant more to them if they'd had the same blood flowing through their veins.

"Th-They just took him…to the imaging department… for X-rays and a scan of his head," she said, unable to keep her voice from cracking.

Nate stepped forward and, putting his arms around her, pulled her to his broad chest. "He's going to be all right, Bria."

"Sam's as tough as nails," Lane Donaldson added. The same age as Sam, Lane had a master's degree in psychology that he used quite successfully as a professional poker player. Bria didn't think she had ever seen the man look less confident.

Ryder McClain, the most easygoing of the group, nodded. "Sam's probably already being a pain in the butt about getting out of here."

"I hope all of you are right," she said, feeling helpless.

"Can I get you something, Bria? A cup of coffee or some water?" T. J. Malloy asked solicitously. He was the most thoughtful of the brothers, so she wasn't the least bit surprised that T.J.'s concern extended to her.

"Get some coffee for all of us, T.J.," Nate commanded, without waiting for her to respond.

"I'll go with you to help carry everything," Jaron Lambert offered, turning to follow T.J. Stopping, he turned back to ask, "Do you want anything else, Bria. Maybe something to eat?"

"Thanks, Jaron, but I'm not hungry. I doubt that I could eat anything even if I was," she said, thankful to have Sam's brothers with her. They treated her like a sister and she was going to miss them terribly once the divorce was final and she was no longer part of their family.

"Come on and sit down," Nate said, guiding her over to a bank of chairs along the far wall. When she sat, he asked, "Did Sam regain consciousness in the ambulance on the way over here?"

She shook her head. "I think he was starting to come around when they took him back to the examination room, but they told me I couldn't stay with him and that the doctor would come out and talk to me when he knew something."

Unable to leave the rodeo they had coordinated to honor their late foster father, the men had sent her to the hospital with Sam, while they attended to dispatching the livestock Sam's company had provided for the various events to the next rodeo on the schedule. She knew it had to be extremely hard for them not to have dropped everything to go with their brother to the hospital, but they had done their duty and seen to Sam's interests when he couldn't.

"Is everything over with for this year's memorial rodeo?" she asked, knowing the bull riding was usually the last scheduled event.

"Yup, we got everything taken care of," Lane said, lowering his lanky frame into one of the chairs. "There's nothing for you to worry about right now, except being here for Sam."

"I wish they would come out and tell us something," Bria said, unable to sit still any longer. She walked over to look down the hall toward the room where they had taken Sam.

What could be taking so long? she wondered as she spotted T.J. and Jaron returning with several cups of coffee. The longer it took to hear something, the more worried she became.

"Still no word?" T.J. asked as he stopped to hand her a cup. He had no sooner gotten the words out, when a man in blue scrubs and a white lab coat entered the waiting area.

"Mrs. Rafferty?" he asked, walking over to her.

As she braced herself for whatever news he came to deliver, Sam's brothers rose to stand with her. "I'm Brianna Rafferty," she said, surprised that her voice sounded strong when her nerves were anything but steady. "Is my hus…is Sam going to be all right?"

"I'm Dr. Bailey, the neurologist on call this evening." His expression gave no indication of what kind of news he had to tell them. "Let's sit down and I'll explain what's going on with your husband." Once they were all seated, he pulled up a chair to sit across from them. "Sam regained consciousness just before we took him to Imaging for the CT scan and X-rays, which is a good sign. And there was no evidence of broken bones."

Apparently sensing she needed support, Nate took her hand in his and asked the question that she couldn't. "Why do I hear a 'but' in your voice, Doc?"

"The scan showed that Sam suffered a severe concussion, but there were no signs of bleeding in his brain, which is good," Dr. Bailey explained. "There is, however, some swelling."

"What does that mean?" Jaron demanded. With his raven hair and dark demeanor, Jaron was the type of man other men rarely had the nerve to cross.

"There may or may not be complications." Dr. Bailey met their worried gazes as he continued, "The next twenty-four hours should tell us if the cerebral edema will get worse. If that happens, we may have to take him into surgery to remove a section of his scull to relieve the pressure."

Bria covered her horrified gasp with her hand.

"I really don't think that's something we'll have to do, Mrs. Rafferty," Dr. Bailey hastily added. "I've been monitoring his condition since he was brought into the E.R. and the swelling doesn't show signs of worsening. But even if that isn't an issue, we'll have to watch for other neurological problems that wouldn't show up on a scan."

"What kinds of problems are we talking about here?" Ryder asked, looking as if he would like to punch something. A rodeo bull rider, normally the man was absolutely fearless. But Bria knew his frustration was a mask for the fear they all felt for Sam.

"With brain injuries there's always the possibility of memory loss, problems with reasoning abilities or a personality change," the doctor answered. "I'm not saying any of those things are inevitable or that they would be permanent if they do present, just that there are those possibilities."

"Dear God, this can't be happening," she said as

tears spilled down her cheeks. Sam was so strong, so self-assured, it was impossible to think that he might end up having problems. That she had played a part in his being injured in any way was almost more than she could bear. But she couldn't live with herself if he had long-lasting problems because she'd chosen today to end their marriage.

Nate protectively put his arm around her shoulders. "When will we be able to see him, Doc?"

"We've put him in the Intensive Care Unit for closer observation and he's resting comfortably. But two of you can go in to see him for a few minutes now, then again every two hours or so." The doctor stood up and shook their hands. "I'll let you know more after I assess his condition in the morning. For now, I'll have one of the nurses direct you to the ICU waiting room upstairs."

As the man walked away, Jaron patted her arm. "It's going to be okay, Bria. Sam will get through this without any of those problems."

"Sam's tougher than anyone I've ever seen," T.J. added. "I have no doubt he'll be up and around in no time."

Lane took a deep breath. "Why don't you and Nate go on up to see him, while the rest of us stake a claim on some space in the ICU waiting area."

On the elevator ride to the third floor, Bria couldn't help wondering how much Sam had told his brothers about their divorce. Knowing him the way she did, he probably hadn't told them any more than he had to.

Bria sighed. She might have decided that she couldn't be his wife anymore, but she wanted to be with him tonight, wanted to help see him through whatever he was facing. But she wasn't entirely certain she should stay either. After all, they were so close to being divorced, she wasn't sure she had the right.

"Nate, maybe I shouldn't be here," she said uncertainly.

Her brother-in-law looked at her as if she might be losing her mind. "Why the hell would you say something like that, Bria?"

"Sam and I are one signature away from being divorced," she said, hating the word. "I'm not sure he will even want me to be here."

Nate shook his head. "It doesn't matter. You don't have that signature yet and until you do, as far as I'm concerned, and I'm pretty sure the state of Texas is in agreement on this, the two of you are still married."

"But—"

"But nothing," he cut her off. "You're still his wife, and until this is over with and Sam is back on his feet, this is where you belong. After that, it will be up to the two of you to sort it out."

She supposed Nate was right. Until the dissolution of their marriage was final and the documents filed at the courthouse, they were still legally married. If medical decisions had to be made on Sam's behalf, she would be the one they turned to for answers. Besides, she wanted to be with him until she knew for certain he was going to be all right.

As they stepped off the elevator and turned to go through the Intensive Care Unit doors, Bria bit her lower lip to keep it from trembling. Even though they were ending their relationship, she still cared deeply for him. She just couldn't live with him anymore. Not after what he had done almost five months ago. She had needed him with her when she lost their baby, not his excuses for being unable to leave his stock-contracting company during a rodeo.

When they checked in at the nurse's desk and were directed to Sam's room, a tear slid down Bria's cheek at the sight of him. There was a swollen lump at his right temple and an ugly bruise ran along his jaw, but to her relief his eyes were open, clear, and she knew immediately that he recognized her and Nate.

"Will you tell these people to give me my clothes back so I can get dressed and get out of here?" he asked impatiently.

"Well, some things never change," Nate said, his smile reflecting the relief Bria felt. "I see that bull didn't knock any of the orneriness out of your sorry hide."

Bria approached the side of the bed and, unable to stop herself from touching him, gently brushed Sam's dark blond hair from his brow. "Does your head hurt, Sam?"

He reached for her hand. "Don't worry, sweetheart. I'm going to be just fine. Just find me some clothes, I'll get dressed and we can go home."

"You really need to stay here for a day or two so they can take care of you and make sure you're going to be all right," she said, taking his hand. The moment her palm touched his, a deep sadness for what could have been tightened her chest.

"I'll rest better in our bed at home," he insisted.

"Hell, I'll even let you play nurse if that's what it takes to get me out of here."

Bria silently met Nate's questioning gaze. Why did Sam keep insisting that they go home together? She had moved out of the ranch house three months ago. And if that hadn't been enough to convince her that something was wrong, his concession to let her nurse him back to health was. Another reason she had felt there was no hope for their marriage was the fact that he had so much pride and self-confidence, he never made her feel as if he truly needed her for anything but making love. If he were himself, he wouldn't even consider allowing her to "play nurse."

"Sam, do you know what month this is?" she asked cautiously.

He frowned as if he thought she might be the one with problems. "It's January. Don't you remember, we celebrated New Year's together just before I left to take a string of bulls to the event in Oklahoma. That was last week. Now, will you stop asking me questions and get me something to wear?"

Her heart felt as if it came up in her throat. The bull-riding event he mentioned had taken place six months ago.

"It's getting late and besides, it's a two-hour drive from here to the ranch. Why don't you stay here tonight, then we'll see if they'll let you go home tomorrow morning." Nate glanced at her again, then finished, "In the meantime, Bria and I will see what we can do about finding your clothes."

"That sounds like a good idea, Sam," she agreed. His

obvious lack of memory bothered her and they needed to speak to the doctor about it right away. "Try to get some rest now. I'm sure we'll be able to deal with everything in the morning."

Sam didn't look happy, but apparently deciding he wasn't going to get his way, he finally nodded. "Nate, could you give me a minute with my wife?"

"Sure thing, bro." Nate nodded toward the hall. "I'll be down in the waiting room with the rest of the guys, Bria."

When Nate left the room, Sam pinned her with his piercing blue gaze. "Are you doing all right? You didn't get too upset, did you?"

Confused, she had no idea why he was asking about her welfare. He was the one who had the accident. "I'm doing okay. But why do you ask?"

"We've been trying to have a baby and when I called you from the bull riding up in Oklahoma the other night you told me you were going to get one of those early home-pregnancy tests at the drugstore," Sam said, looking hopeful as he gave her hand a gentle squeeze. "Were we successful, sweetheart? Are you pregnant?"

A cold sinking feeling settled in the pit of her stomach at his mention of their trying to start a family. He didn't remember that she had not only become pregnant, she had miscarried in her seventh week. That had been almost six months ago and had ended up being the last straw in making her decision to file for divorce. Something was definitely wrong if he had no recollection of the past several months' tumultuous events.

"No, I'm not pregnant," she said, determined to talk

to the neurologist as soon as possible. "Now, get some rest and I'll be in a little later to check on you."

"Don't worry, sweetheart," Sam said, smiling. "We haven't been trying that long. I'm sure you'll be pregnant within another month or so."

Unsure if she could respond without bursting into tears or reminding him that he would have had to be home more for her to become pregnant again, she simply nodded and turned to leave.

"Aren't you going to give me a good-night kiss, sweetheart?" he asked, still holding her hand.

"I...uh... They won't let me take down the bed rail," she said, thinking fast. Kissing the tip of her index finger, she pressed it to his lips. "You need to get some rest so they'll let you out of here soon. Try to get some sleep, Sam."

He gave her a grin that never failed to cause her heart to skip a beat. "It's going to be damn hard to do without you here beside me."

She once again had to bite her tongue to keep from pointing out that sleeping without her hadn't seemed to be a problem for him when he was traveling from one rodeo to another with his livestock-contracting company. But as she stared down at his handsome face, she decided that now wasn't the time to get into how lonely she had been without him, how many times she had asked him to cut back on the travel or to remind him that some time ago, he had reached his goal of being independently wealthy and didn't need to work if he didn't want to. His smile was playing havoc with her resolve and she needed to put distance between them in order to regain her perspective.

"Good night, Sam."

Some things never changed, she thought as she walked down the hall to the waiting area. The sun rose in the east each morning. The ocean rushed to shore. And Sam Rafferty could make her knees wobble with nothing more than his sexy-as-sin smile.

"I really don't see any other way around it, Bria," Nate insisted, shaking his head. "You're going to have to move back into the ranch house with Sam until he regains his memory."

After finally getting a chance to talk to the doctor the day after the accident, Sam's brothers and Bria had decided to get a good night's sleep, then meet in the hospital cafeteria this morning for coffee as they discussed how best to handle Sam's recovery.

Dr. Bailey had informed them that after staying in the hospital for observation the past forty-eight hours, Sam had been cleared to go home, but that he was suffering from post-concussion syndrome. That was the reason he had forgotten everything that had happened during the past six months. The doctor had assured them that the condition was most likely temporary and would clear up on its own in a few weeks with Sam recovering most, if not all, of his memory. But until then he might suffer with headaches and spells of dizziness and shouldn't become overly stressed or worried. And that was what brought them together to discuss the current dilemma. It was imperative that someone be with him at all times until he was fully recovered.

"Can't one of you stay with him?" she asked, looking at each man in turn. "Or maybe hire someone to oversee his care?"

"Hiring a nurse would be out of the question," T.J. said, adamantly shaking his head. "That would just piss him off and traumatize some poor nurse after she figured out he's like a grizzly with a sore paw when he can't do things for himself."

"Any one of us could arrange to stay with him, but that wouldn't solve the problem of Sam not getting overly stressed," Lane said as if weighing his words carefully. "He doesn't remember that the two of you were in the process of getting a divorce, let alone that you moved out. And right now that's information he doesn't need to hear." Being a professional poker player, the man was a master at strategy and logic. At the moment, he was doing a fine job of using both to wear her down.

"You know we would do it for Sam in a heartbeat, but we aren't who he's going to expect—or want—to be with him," Ryder pointed out.

"But all my things are in Dallas," she said, feeling trapped. "Don't you think he'll notice there are none of my personal effects in the ranch house? No clothes. No pictures of my family."

She knew it was a weak argument, but how was she supposed to get on with rebuilding her life if she had to go back to Sugar Creek Ranch and all the problems that had caused her to leave in the first place? And especially when the man she would be living with didn't remember that those problems had become insurmountable.

"We all have trucks and strong backs," T.J. said, shrugging.

Jaron nodded. "We can have you moved back into the house in nothing flat."

Sighing, Bria knew what they said made perfect sense, but it still didn't make it any easier to accept defeat. She had just started to get used to the idea that she wouldn't be living the life she had planned when she married Sam. For three years, she had envisioned herself as a stay-at-home wife and mother to the big family they had planned to have. Then after making the painful decision to leave him, she had to start thinking about re-entering the workforce and building a career.

"If I do this, it's only temporary." She felt as if she was taking a huge step back from the course she had set for herself three months ago.

"Got it," Nate said.

"I'm starting a new job as a marketing consultant for one of the department stores in Dallas in a few weeks when they start to expand their women's clothing line, and I can't afford to miss out on this opportunity," she stressed. "I'm lucky they allowed me the time to get the divorce finalized and my feet back under me before I start the job. I'm not going to ask for more."

"I'm certain Sam will have his memory back by then," Lane assured her.

"And I wouldn't want everything moved back to the ranch," she warned them.

"Just tell us what you want out of your apartment and

we'll make sure that it's in the house by the time you and Sam get home," Ryder said, smiling.

Nate checked his watch. "We'd better get moving. They're going to discharge Sam in a couple hours. That doesn't give us a lot time to get to Dallas and then out to the ranch before you two get there."

"Just get my clothes and shoes out of the closet," she said, resigned. "I'll go into town and buy whatever else I need."

"Are you sure that's it?" Ryder asked, frowning. "Won't you need your under—"

"Positive," she interrupted. She wasn't about to have them bring anything else from her apartment. The thought of five men going through her underwear drawer to pack a box of panties, bras and nightgowns to bring to the ranch just wasn't the least bit appealing.

Giving Nate the address of her apartment in Dallas, she handed him her key. "After you get my clothes, go to the manager's office and tell her to hold my mail until I can get back up that way in a week or so to pick it up."

"How are you going to manage getting away from Sam for the hour-and-a-half drive to get up there?" Jaron asked, frowning.

"I'm sure Sam will have a follow-up appointment with the neurologist sometime within the next couple of weeks." She gave them all a warning look as she started to get up. "If I'm going to stay with him until he's recovered, one of you will be taking him to the doctor here in Waco while I drive to Dallas to see about my apartment and get my mail." Before they could come up with an excuse to get out of it, she added, "You owe me that much."

She wasn't at all surprised when all five of them rose to their feet as she stood up. She had known them almost as long as she had known Sam, and from the moment they met her, they had all treated her as if she was the sister they never had. Hank Calvert had not only helped them straighten out their youthful problems and set them on a course to become highly successful, extremely wealthy men, he had taught them manners and respect, as well as instilled in them a strong sense of family.

"Thanks for doing this for Sam," Nate said, giving her a brotherly kiss on the cheek. "We really appreciate it, Bria."

When they walked her to the elevator, each man hugged her and assured her they would see her at the ranch. As Bria watched them walk toward the hospital's main exit, she couldn't help dreading the upcoming weeks. How on earth was she going to act as if everything was all right?

Sam was the same man who worked constantly, couldn't take the time for them as a couple and was never there for her when she needed him most. She had tried to tell him time after time what was wrong with their marriage—the reasons she was so unhappy and why she wanted them to return to the way things had been between them before they married. But all he would say was that everything he did was for her and their future. She finally came to the conclusion that no matter how successful and wealthy he became, it was never going to be enough. When he waited an entire day before he came home to check on her after she lost their baby, she knew she couldn't go on with the way things were. Even when she needed him, he put his business first. Now, she was going back to the same situation.

Stepping onto the elevator, she pushed the button for the third floor. No, nothing had changed. Sam was still an incurable workaholic and without a doubt her biggest weakness. He always had been and unfortunately for her, she suspected that would never change.

Two

As Bria steered her SUV onto the road leading up to the ranch house she had called home for the past three years, she glanced over at Sam. He hadn't had much to say on the drive from the hospital and she wondered if he was trying to remember events from the past six months.

"Is something wrong?" she asked.

"I don't remember us buying this SUV," he finally said. "How long have we had it?"

"About three months," she answered, deciding to be honest, but omitting the fact that she had bought the Explorer after she moved away from the ranch.

As of yet, Sam hadn't asked a lot of questions after being told that he had a form of amnesia, and she was extremely grateful. She wasn't in the habit of lying to anyone, especially to Sam. For one thing, their relationship had always been based on honesty and trust and although their marriage was at an end, it didn't mean that had to change. And for another, not telling Sam the truth wouldn't do a thing to help him regain his memory. The doctor had advised that it would be better to let Sam remember the events of the past six months on his own and not inundate him with facts that might prove stressful and possibly impede his recovery.

"It seems pretty nice," he said, looking around the interior of the vehicle.

She nodded. "I like it."

"Did we get it in anticipation of a baby?" he asked, turning to look in the back. "Looks like there should be plenty of room for a car seat."

"No."

That was the second time he had mentioned them trying to become pregnant, and it wasn't any easier to hear this time than it had been the other night at the hospital. Every time she thought about the baby she had miscarried almost five months ago, her chest tightened from the crushing loss, as well as the hurt and anger she still felt at him for not being there for her when she had needed his strength and support. He had chosen work over her and the loss of their baby, and that was something she didn't think she would ever be able to get past.

She jumped when Sam reached over and placed his index finger to her mouth to stop her from nibbling on her lower lip. "Sweetheart, if you don't stop that, there won't be anything left for me to kiss."

Hoping to change the subject, she took a deep breath and nodded toward the house. "It looks like your brothers are here to visit with you while I go into town to pick up a few things."

"I don't need a damn babysitter," he said, clearly irritated by the thought.

"This isn't up for debate, Sam." She shook her head. At times, his pride was one of the most infuriating things about him. "You're not calling the shots here— I am. The doctor said someone needed to be with you at all times and that's exactly what's going to happen. You might as well accept that."

"We'll see," he said, indicating that he wasn't going to make things easy.

When she parked the SUV, Sam got out of the truck before she could tell him to wait until she made sure he was steady enough to make it to the house. Pointing to the five men on the back porch having a beer, he called, "Hey, grab me one of those."

"Don't you dare," Bria warned them as she closed the driver's door. "The doctor said no alcoholic beverages." Coming around the front of the Explorer, she asked, "Do you feel all right? You aren't dizzy, are you?"

"I'm not a hothouse flower, Bria," he said impatiently. "Other than not being able to remember the past six months, I'm fine. I could have driven us home and I don't see why I can't have a beer. It doesn't have *that* much alcohol in it."

"Let me tell you something, Sam Rafferty," she said sternly. "You're going to do exactly what the doctor outlined in the release instructions or I swear I'll—"

"Do you have any idea how sexy you are when you start pitching a hissy fit?" he interrupted, tenderly touching her cheek. The gesture and his wicked grin sent a tiny thrill straight up her spine, distracting her. She had missed his touch and playfulness. It wasn't something she had seen a lot of since he started the Sugar Creek Rodeo Company right after they married. "As soon as my brothers leave I'll show you what it does to me."

Bria forced herself to ignore the tremendous yearning that coursed through her. Lovemaking had been the one area of their marriage that was everything it should have been—at least it had been when he wasn't traveling from one rodeo to another. But just because Sam didn't remember they were calling it quits was no excuse for her to forget and give in to the temptation of being held by him once again. Leaving had been hard enough the first time, making love with him now would only make it doubly so when he regained his memory and she had to leave again.

"There won't be any of *that,* either," she said as much for her own benefit as it was for his. "You're not supposed to get overly excited or stressed."

"Sweetheart, making love isn't stressful," he said, putting his arm around her shoulders as they walked toward the back-porch steps. "It's actually a great stress reliever, not to mention just plain fun."

Her cheeks heated. "Shh. Your brothers will hear."

"I'm pretty sure they wouldn't be all that shocked," he teased. "I think they know married folks carry on like that."

Sam suddenly stopped walking and she could tell

that he was having a problem by the way he leaned on her for support. "Nate! I need help! Sam's dizzy!"

Nate and the other four men were down the steps and at Sam's side in a flash. "Let's get you into the house, bro," Nate said, lifting Sam's arm to his shoulders to relieve the weight from Bria.

"I can make it on my own steam," Sam insisted. A muscle along his jaw worked furiously, indicating that he was fighting with everything he had to will the vertigo away.

Shaking her head at his foolish pride, Bria let out a frustrated sigh. "I'm going to let you all watch him while I go to town to buy groceries and some other necessities."

"You are coming back, aren't you?" Nate asked a little too quickly.

"Why wouldn't she come back?" Sam frowned. "She lives here. Where else would she go?"

"Yes, I'll be back," she promised, ducking from beneath his arm. "I assume you took care of everything while I was at the hospital picking up Sam?"

"All done," T.J. answered.

"What's going on?" Sam demanded, looking from her to his brothers. "If somebody doesn't tell me what the hell's going on, I'm going to—"

"You can be pretty darned ornery when you don't feel good," Nate said, shrugging.

"Bria might decide to take off for parts unknown if you don't follow doctor's orders," Lane added. "If I were you, I'd do what she tells you to do."

When Sam seemed to accept their explanation, Bria

breathed a sigh of relief. Very many mistakes like the one Nate had just made and they would have to tell Sam the truth before he could remember it on his own.

"And don't worry about our getting everything done," Ryder said, checking his watch. "We took care of getting the livestock loaded and sent on to the Del Rio rodeo. I'm going to hit the road and head on down there now. I'm supposed to work this one anyway, and it won't be a big deal for me to oversee the wranglers."

"Thanks, Ryder," Sam said. "I appreciate it."

"No need to thank me," Ryder said, shaking his head. "You'd do the same for me if I needed help."

"We'll be down in a couple of days to help out," T.J. said as Ryder turned to walk to his truck.

"Are we getting together for my birthday on Sunday, Bria?" Jaron looked hopeful. "You know how much I love your apple pie."

"Of course," she said, smiling.

She was glad Jaron mentioned his upcoming birthday. Planning his birthday dinner would give her something to concentrate on besides how much she wished things could be different for her and Sam. Besides, she loved holding family celebrations, and with all the men coming back for the weekend, it would give her a break from the pressure she anticipated being under while taking care of Sam.

Apparently satisfied that everything was as it should be, Sam nodded toward her SUV. "Drive careful, sweetheart."

Walking to her Explorer, Bria wondered how she was going to make it through the next few weeks without losing her mind. Sam was far too perceptive not to pick up on every little slip, and it was just a matter of time before he realized that things between them were vastly different from what he remembered. Unfortunately, explaining that their marriage was over and why would do nothing but add to the stress he was already under from just trying to recall the past several months.

As she drove from the ranch yard, she sighed heavily. How had she managed to get herself into such a complicated situation? But more important than that, how on earth was she going to get herself out of it and remain on the course she had set for herself three months ago?

With their housekeeper and part-time cook, Rosa, off visiting her sister in San Antonio for a couple of weeks, Bria was in the kitchen cooking supper, while Sam sat in the family room pretending to watch the local evening news. She had insisted that he take it easy and he was trying, but it was damn hard to do. He wasn't used to being idle and having to sit around with nothing to do made him feel like a worthless slug. He was accustomed to doing what a man was supposed to do—work hard and make a good living for his wife and the family they were planning to have.

Thinking about his stock-contracting business, he smiled. He was proud of the fact that he had started from scratch and built the Sugar Creek Rodeo Company to the level that he could retire right now without any worries for the rest of his days. But he wasn't of a mind to do that. As Hank always said, everyone needed a purpose. Sam's mission in life was to work hard so that Bria would never want for anything, never have to worry where money for their next meal would come from. Unlike what his biological father had done for his mother, Sam intended to see that his wife got whatever her heart desired.

As he looked around the room, he tried to remember the last time he had been home for more than a couple of days at a time. It was frustrating as hell not to recall even the simplest of memories, not to mention it was taking a big toll on his pride. Showing any kind of weakness never had been his style. But the fact that Bria was witness to his most recent limitations made the whole situation doubly humiliating.

He was supposed to be strong and capable—the man who took care of her, not the other way around. Unless he missed his guess, she was having just as hard of a time seeing him this way as he was of being the husband with some major limitations and no recent memories.

From the time she had come into the ICU to see him the night of the accident, Bria had been aloof, and their conversations, what few they'd had, were awkward at best. Had the fact that he had been hurt caused her to think of him as being inept? Or had she been there to see the bull run him down and was still traumatized by witnessing the accident?

He tried to think, but like everything else that had happened recently, he couldn't remember. "Bria, could you come here a minute?"

When she walked in from the kitchen, she looked absolutely beautiful. A few strands of auburn hair had escaped the confines of her ponytail and her cheeks were delightfully pink from the heat of cooking supper.

"Is everything all right?" she asked, a look of concern in her pretty green eyes.

"I'm fine." He gave her what he hoped was a reassuring smile. "I was just wondering if you were at the rodeo. Did you see what happened?"

She nodded. "You were…distracted when the bull got loose. But I thought your brothers told you all about that while I was in town this afternoon."

"They did." Frowning, he shook his head. "I just can't believe I was that careless. I'm normally real cautious around the bulls and especially that brindle. He's as mean as a rattlesnake. Do you know what had my attention just before the accident happened?"

"They didn't tell you?"

"No."

He watched her take a deep breath before she looked down at her tightly clasped hands.

"I had just arrived and you were watching me."

"That doesn't sound like me. I never let myself get distracted while I'm working with livestock." He ran his hand over the tension building at the back of his neck. "And normally when you come to one of the rodeos, you get there well before the events start, not when they're almost over. Why were you running so late?"

"You know how bad traffic can be on I-35." She glanced over her shoulder into the kitchen. "I really need to check on the spaghetti."

"We'll talk about it over supper," he said, nodding.

When Bria disappeared into the kitchen, he was more

confused than ever. Why had he been watching her instead of what he had been doing? And why did she seem so nervous about it? Did she somehow feel responsible for the accident? Was she feeling guilty?

That didn't make any sense. It was his fault he hadn't been paying attention, not hers.

When a dull pain suddenly reverberated through his head, Sam groaned and shut his eyes. A vision of Bria standing on the front porch with tears streaming down her face immediately flashed behind his closed eyes, then in a matter of seconds it disappeared along with the headache.

His eyes snapped open. Could that have actually happened during the past several months? A knot formed in the pit of his stomach. In all their years together, he could never remember seeing Bria look so unhappy, so filled with sadness. What could have possibly caused her to look as if her heart was breaking?

Over the past year or two, she had let it be known on more than one occasion that she would like him to be home with her more. But of all their arguments about the time he spent out on the road with the rodeo company, he could never remember her being *that* miserable. Had things between them escalated to that point? Or had something else happened to cause her such heartache and he just couldn't remember?

Lost in his disturbing thoughts, it took a moment for Sam to realize Bria was standing beside his chair with her hand on his arm. "Sam, are you all right?"

"I…uh, yeah," he said, not sure if the image had been a fragment of recovered memory or his imagination working overtime. Taking her by the hand, he pulled her down to sit on his lap. "I'm fine."

"This isn't a good idea, Sam." She placed her hand on his chest as if she intended to get up, then stopped abruptly. "Something *is* wrong. Your heart is racing."

Wrapping his arms around her waist, he kissed the tip of her nose. "You know that always happens when I'm close to you, sweetheart."

He didn't want to ask her about the vision just yet. Just the thought of Bria actually experiencing that kind of emotional pain was gut-wrenching.

"Do you feel like coming into the kitchen for dinner or would you rather I bring a tray in here for you?" she asked, her gaze not quite meeting his.

"What's wrong, Bria?" he asked. "And don't tell me 'nothing.' I know you well enough to tell when something is bothering you."

"I…guess I'm just worried," she said slowly, as if choosing her words carefully.

Bringing his hand up, he gently brushed a strand of auburn hair from her soft cheek. "I'm here. My muscles are still a little sore, but I'm okay—we're okay. And once I convince the doctor to release me to go back to work, everything will be back to normal."

Lowering his head, he started to cover her mouth with his, but to his surprise she pulled away from him and stood up. "Of course, everything will go back to the way it was. Why wouldn't it?" Her eyes sparkled with anger. "You'll go back to traveling from one rodeo to another with the livestock and I'll—" She stopped abruptly, took a deep breath, then to his utter bewilderment, she smiled. "I'll be just fine. Now, do you feel like coming into the kitchen to eat or do you want me to bring your supper to you in here?"

Sam frowned. "Bria, what's going on?"

He had never known her to switch gears quite that fast. If he didn't know her better, he would swear she was trying to hide something from him. But that didn't make any sense. Their relationship had always been based on honesty and sharing whatever was on their minds. With the exception of his life before he and Nate entered the foster care system—a life filled with mistakes he never intended to share with her or anyone else—they knew everything about each other. There wasn't a single thing he could think of that she might feel the need to keep from him.

"Don't mind me. It's been a long day and I'm tired, that's all." She motioned toward the kitchen. "But I do need to know where you want to eat. If you'd like to finish watching the news—"

"Kitchen," he interrupted, slowly rising to his feet. "I wasn't paying much attention to the news, anyway. Since I can't remember what's been going on in the world for the past six months, there isn't a lot of it that makes sense right now."

As he followed Bria, Sam couldn't help smiling. Even after three years of marriage, he loved watching the sexy sway of her shapely backside. It never failed to cause his heart to pound and his temperature to rise. This evening she looked exceptionally appealing in her summery pink sundress with skinny little straps that kept falling off her shoulders.

His smile suddenly turned to an all-out grin. Although he wasn't used to being idle and viewed taking off work as a complete waste, he had a feeling that his forced downtime might not be that bad after all. Bria had been after him for the past year or so to slow down and spend more time with her and he saw no reason why they couldn't enjoy his unexpected vacation for as long as it lasted. In fact, it might be just what they needed to make the baby they had both been anticipating.

The moment Sam stepped up behind her where she stood at the sink, Bria felt a warm tingling sensation course from the top of her head all the way to her toes even before he wrapped his arms around her waist to pull her back against his solid frame. The chemistry between them had always been that way. Sam just had to walk into a room and all her senses went on high alert.

"Why aren't you putting those in the dishwasher?" he asked, nodding toward the dishes she was washing. His warm breath feathering over the side of her neck sent a wave of longing straight through her.

She would have liked nothing better than to turn in his arms and have him kiss her until her knees gave way. But falling back into old habits now was not going to help her rebuild her life once Sam regained his memory and she left Sugar Creek Ranch for good. She needed to keep that uppermost in her mind.

Concentrating on the plate she was washing to keep from doing something she knew she would later regret, Bria shrugged. "Since Rosa is visiting her sister and no one's been here for the past few days, there really weren't enough dishes to warrant using the dishwasher. Besides, after we hired her to do the cooking and cleaning, the only time I get to be domestic is when one of the guys has a birthday and I make a celebratory dinner. I've missed doing things like cooking and washing a few dishes. It makes me feel useful and needed."

"I can think of something a lot more fun for an after-dinner activity that will make you feel just as needed," he said, his tone low and intimate. He brushed her long hair aside to slowly nibble kisses from just below her ear, down her neck to her bare shoulder. "Why don't you put the rest of the dishes in the dishwasher and go upstairs with me. I can't remember the last time I made love to you, but it feels like it's been a while."

She wasn't certain if it was the temptation of once again being loved by Sam, of experiencing his tenderness and the mastery of his touch, or the fear that she wouldn't be able to resist him, but Bria's heart skipped erratically, then took off beating as if she had run a marathon. "I don't think that would be in either of our best interests," she said truthfully, pulling the thin strap of her sundress back on top of her shoulder.

He stopped his sensual assault and turned her to face him. "You want to explain that?"

The frown on his handsome face was a good indication that whatever explanation she came up with needed to be reasonable and something that he would have no trouble accepting. Thinking quickly, she smiled. "The doctor told both of us that you need to take it easy for a few more days. I'm going to see to it that's exactly what you do."

"Okay," he said, his grin wicked. "I'll just lie there and let you make love to me."

Staring up at him, she was reminded of how things had been during the early days of their marriage—the playfulness, the inability to keep their hands off each other. That had been before the Sugar Creek Rodeo Company had become a resounding success and Sam had become obsessed with making it bigger and better than any of his competitors.

"I've got a better idea," she said, turning back to the sink when he started to lower his head for a kiss. "Why don't I finish the dishes and then we can go out onto the porch and watch the sunset together."

"Seriously?" She could hear the frustration in his voice and knew that he wasn't going to give up easily. "You'd rather watch the sun go down than to go upstairs and try to make a baby with me?"

Her chest tightened with the mention of the baby they had both wanted. He couldn't remember and she couldn't tell him that there had been a baby—a baby they had both wanted and that she had lost. Nor could she tell him how much his absence had affected her when she'd had the miscarriage.

"Sam, it's not a good time—"

"Ah, so that's what the deal is," he said, his tone suddenly filled with understanding. "Why didn't you just come out and tell me you're having your period? You've never been shy about that with me before."

She had intended to explain that it wasn't a good time to discuss starting a family while he was recovering from the concussion, but his misconception would keep her from having to make excuses for at least a few more days. Besides, by not correcting his assumption, she wasn't exactly lying to him. She knew he probably wouldn't see it that way, but it really was best for both of them.

"I had other things on my mind," she said evasively. Deciding it was time for a change of subject, she added, "I'll be finished with the dishes in a few more minutes. Why don't you go on out to the porch and get comfortable in the swing."

"Since it looks like that's the most excitement I'm going to have for the evening, I guess I might as well." He kissed the side of her neck, then releasing her, started toward the back door. "Don't be long."

Bria waited until Sam had closed the kitchen door before resting her forearms on the edge of the sink to sag against it. By the time Sam regained his memory, she was going to be thoroughly exhausted from dancing around the truth, as well as fighting the temptation he posed. No matter how disillusioned and angry she had been with him over the past several months, no matter how many times she told herself that she couldn't live with a man who was never there for her, she still wanted him.

Deciding that she was going to need reinforcement, she quickly finished washing the last of the dishes and walked into the study to pick up the phone. When her sister answered on the second ring, Bria said, "Mariah, I need your help. Get down to the ranch as soon as you can. And plan on staying a couple of days."

* * *

"I thought you told me you'd only be a few minutes," Sam said when Bria walked out onto the porch. "I was just about to come looking for you, sweetheart."

Instead of sitting beside him on the swing as he thought she would, she walked over to stand by the porch rail. "I was on the phone with my sister."

"How is Mariah?" Sam asked, unable to remember the last time he had seen his sister-in-law. Five years younger than Bria, the two sisters were as close as he and his brothers.

"She's coming down from Amarillo for the weekend." Bria turned to give him a smile. "She offered to help me make dinner for Jaron's birthday."

Sam wasn't the least bit surprised that Mariah planned to attend the birthday dinner for his brother. Aside from the fact that the vivacious brunette attended all the birthday celebrations Bria arranged for him and his brothers, it was no secret that Mariah had a huge crush on Jaron. That his brother thought of her as off-limits because she was Bria's sister and ten years younger than himself was no secret either.

"It'll be good to see her again," Sam said, meaning it. He liked his sister-in-law and thought she would be good for Jaron—help settle him down. But it wasn't his place to interfere. That was Jaron's business, and Hank had taught them all not to stick their noses in where they didn't belong.

"Why don't you come over here and sit down?" he asked when Bria continued to stand by the rail.

She hesitated a moment, then slowly walked over to

lower herself onto the porch swing next to him. "You looked comfortable and I didn't want to disturb you."

Sam released a frustrated breath. "Dammit, Bria, that run-in with the brindle bull didn't turn me into an invalid. I may still have a couple of aching muscles, but give me some credit. I'm made of stronger stuff than that."

"I know, but—"

"But nothing," he interrupted. He moved his outstretched arm from the back of the swing to put it around her shoulders and pull her to his side. "You're my wife. This is where I want you and where you belong—right here in my arms."

Lowering his head before she could find another lame excuse not to kiss him, Sam covered her soft lips with his and savored the sweet taste of the woman he cared for more than he ever dreamed was possible. At first she stiffened in his arms as if she meant to pull away from him, then, whimpering, she put her arms around his shoulders and kissed him back like a woman greeting her soldier returning home from war.

Not one to try solving the mysteries of a woman's inner thoughts, Sam relegated her reaction to the back of his mind as he deepened the kiss. There would be plenty of time to ponder why Bria had been running hot and cold all day and why she was kissing him now with a desperation that robbed him of breath. At the moment, she was in his arms and that was all that mattered.

As he stroked her tongue with his, she tangled her fingers in the hair at the nape of his neck and pressed herself closer. His body's reaction was not only predictable, it was immediate. He was hotter than hell and aching to sink himself deep inside her in two seconds flat. But their timing was lousy. It wasn't a good time for her and as much as he hated to admit it, he still wasn't feeling a hundred percent. And he never gave her less than a hundred and ten percent of himself when they made love.

"Sweetheart…" he said, reluctantly breaking the kiss. He took a big gulp of much-needed air before he could continue. "I think we'd better slow this down just a little. You can't make love right now and I'd really rather not have to freeze my ass off taking a cold shower."

Bria blinked as if coming out of a trance, then quickly pushed herself away from him, jumped to her feet and started toward the door. "I can't…do this," she said, her voice cracking as if she was on the verge of tears. "It's just not…going to work."

Sam quickly got up to follow her and question her about what she had meant, but the moment he rose to his feet, a wave of dizziness swept over him, followed quickly by a sharp pain that seemed to ricochet inside his skull. Groaning, he sank back onto the wooden swing as an image crossed his mind of another time Bria had said those same words as she tearfully walked away from him.

"Sam, what's wrong?" she asked, rushing back over to kneel in front of him.

"I'm just a little…dizzy," he said, trying desperately to remember why she had been upset with him. But as quickly as the scrap of memory came to him, it was gone along with the wave of light-headedness and the pain in his head.

"I think it would be best for you to be in bed," she said, lightly touching his cheek with her fingertips. "You've been up since I brought you home early this afternoon and you need to rest. You're still weak from—"

"Dammit, Bria. I told you, I'm not some hothouse flower." He knew she was concerned, but she couldn't have made him feel more inadequate if she had tried.

"Please, let me help you to bed," she pleaded. "If you won't do it for yourself, then please do it for me—for my peace of mind."

Sam could tell that she wasn't going to give him a moment's peace until he did what she wanted and, whether he liked it or not, he was exhausted. Not willing to verbally admit that he was giving in, he simply gave her a short nod and slowly rose to his feet.

She was only trying to do what she thought was best for him, and he appreciated that. But it didn't help his pride one damn bit. A man wasn't supposed to appear weak and frail in the eyes of his woman. His real father might have thrived on that sort of thing, but he didn't. That Bria viewed him that way now was quite possibly the most humiliating thing that he had ever had to endure. And he vowed right then and there, if it was within his power to prevent it, it would never happen again.

Three

After a sleepless night in one of the guest bedrooms, Bria was up before daylight. Being back at Sugar Creek Ranch was bittersweet for her. She loved the big sprawling, two-story home Sam had built when they first got married, loved to sit on the porch with him to watch the sunset and listen to the crickets chirp and an occasional coyote howl as night descended.

That's why she had become so upset when Sam kissed her. It reminded her too much of the early days of their marriage when they had spent every moment they could together on that swing, watching sunsets as they shared their hopes and dreams and made plans for their future. But that had been before Sam's stock-contracting company had become so successful and he started traveling all over the country supplying livestock for the various rodeos. In the past two years, more times than not, she had sat on the porch by herself to watch the sun sink behind the ridge surrounding the ranch, waited for Sam's nightly phone call from whatever town he was in to tell her good-night and slept alone in that big bed upstairs in the master suite.

Not having to worry about money or paying bills was nice, but it wasn't everything. Having her husband home with her, to talk to about how their day had gone and to hold her at night would have meant far more to her than going from being financially secure to being independently wealthy.

Sighing, she turned her attention back to the sizzling bacon she was frying for his breakfast. When she'd checked on him earlier, he was still sleeping peacefully. She fleetingly wondered if he had awakened some time during the night and noticed that she wasn't lying next to him. She doubted it. If he had, she was certain he would have come looking for her.

As she placed the crispy strips of bacon on a plate, then scrambled a couple of eggs, she couldn't help worrying. Last night Sam had been so exhausted, he hadn't noticed that she had gone to bed in another room. But as he started feeling better and regained his strength, he was bound to question why she wasn't sleeping with him. What was she going to tell him when he did?

She wasn't going to lie, but she couldn't tell him the truth either. Mentioning that they had been in the process of getting a divorce when the accident occurred certainly fell into the category of things that would cause him stress. But trying to do everything she could to keep his stress level down was driving hers right off the chart.

When she put the finishing touches on Sam's breakfast and placed it on a tray, she decided not to think about it until she had to. Maybe by the end of the day an idea would present itself that would adequately explain why she was going to bed down the hall. She wouldn't allow herself to contemplate what would happen if it didn't.

Carrying the tray upstairs, she decided Sam probably wasn't going to be overly happy about her serving him breakfast in bed. No doubt he would misinterpret the gesture and think she viewed him as feeble or some other such nonsense. His pride and self-confidence were stronger than anyone's she had ever known and two of the many things that had drawn her to him in the beginning. Unfortunately, as time went on, those very qualities had become a huge obstacle and one of the main reasons she had felt she had no other choice but to leave him.

But his accident had changed that—if only temporarily. For the first time in the five years they had been together, she actually felt as if Sam needed her as more than the object of his affections. It was just a shame that the feeling had to come at the end of their marriage, instead of being an integral part of their relationship from the beginning.

When she opened the bedroom door, Bria placed the tray of food on the dresser then walked over to the side of the bed to wake him. "Sam? Would you like to get up? I brought your breakfast."

Before she realized that he was already awake, he reached up to wrap his arms around her waist and pull her down on top of him. "I'm perfectly capable of walking the distance to the kitchen to eat," he said, rolling them to their sides to face each other. "But what I want for breakfast isn't found in the kitchen. She's right here in my arms."

The smoldering light in his dark blue eyes stole her breath and caused a flutter of anticipation deep in her lower belly. "I—I thought we settled this yesterday evening. I told you it's not a—"

"I know, it's not a good time." He gave her a lazy grin. "But making love isn't just about having sex, sweetheart." He brushed her lips with his. "It's also kissing." He slid his hand beneath the tail of her yellow T-shirt. "And touching," he finished as his mouth covered hers at the same time he cupped her breast in his callused palm.

A lazy heat began to flow through Bria as Sam deepened the kiss to explore and tease with a thoroughness that caused her heart to skip several beats. She knew she was playing a fool's game and that nothing but heartache would come of allowing him to continue. She told herself that he thought they were still a couple and short of telling him about the divorce, she didn't have a lot of choice. But deep down she knew better. She simply loved the way he was making her feel.

Fortunately for her, his cell phone on the bedside table rang at the same moment Sam moved his hand to unfasten the front clasp of her bra. As he cursed and reached for the phone to quiet the incessant noise, Bria seized the opportunity to roll to the opposite side of the mattress and get out of bed.

She watched him check the caller ID before taking the call. "Your timing sucks swamp water, little brother," Sam growled impatiently. "This had better be good."

While he reassured Nate that he was feeling a lot better now that he was out of the hospital and back home, Bria walked over to pick up the breakfast tray. "Your brother was up earlier than usual," she said, carrying it over to the bed as Sam ended the call and placed the phone back on the nightstand.

"I'm betting he hasn't gone to sleep yet." Sam shook his head. "I've told him that he needs to use some of that fortune he's won riding the rough stock to buy a ranch, then find himself a good woman like I did and settle down. But that wild streak in him is a mile wide."

Bria couldn't argue with Sam's assessment of his younger brother. She loved her brother-in-law dearly, but for as long as she had known him, Nate's escapades with women had been legendary. He loved the ladies and they loved him.

"I told you I could make it to the kitchen on my own steam," Sam said, scowling at the tray as he started to get out of bed.

"Last night was an indication that you still need to take it easy," she said, handing him the tray to keep from dumping it in his lap as she would have liked. "And whether you like it or not, I enjoy doing things for you."

His stubborn pride was beginning to grate on her already frayed nerves, but she didn't want to upset him. The whole point of her moving back to the ranch temporarily was to keep him calm and hopefully speed up the recovery of his memory, not prolong the amnesia. The sooner he remembered the events of the past six months, the sooner she could get on with the rest of her life. And if she kept reminding herself of that fact, she might be able to avoid throttling him.

"What happened out on the porch last night was a fluke," he groused, clearly irritated that she had brought up the incident. He tried to hand the tray back to her, but she ignored him. "I'm going to take a shower and get dressed, then—"

"Please, Sam, I don't want to argue." Reaching for the pillows, she took her time propping them up between him and the headboard in an effort to stay calm. If she didn't, she just might take one of them and bop him with it. "Sit back, enjoy your breakfast and then take a shower."

When he set the tray on the bed, then stood up, anger and resentment threatened to put an end to her resolution not to argue with him. "I wish just once you would let me feel like I'm your wife and let me do something for you. It would be a refreshing change to feel as if you needed me for more than making love," she said before she could stop herself.

He frowned. "What the hell do you mean by that?"

Bria knew that if she didn't put some distance between them she would end up saying more than he was ready to hear. "I'll take this to the kitchen," she said, picking up the tray. "I'd ask you to wait until I return before you get into the shower in case you become light-headed, but you wouldn't listen and I'm tired of trying to convince you to follow doctor's orders."

"I don't need—"

"Save it, Sam," she said as she walked to the door to take his breakfast downstairs. "I've already heard it more times than I care to count."

Standing in the shower, Sam frowned as he tried to figure out why Bria was so upset. What had she meant by that comment about wanting him to let her feel like his wife?

He could remember her mentioning it a few times in the past couple of years, but he hadn't understood it then any more than he did now. Did fussing over him make her feel more like a wife? Or did she think she wanted him to sit flat on his rear and let her do everything for him?

If so, she was in for a huge letdown. He wasn't going to let any woman take care of him. That wasn't what a real man did.

From the moment he knew he wanted to marry her he had worked his ass off to make sure he could provide her with the best life had to offer. He had done everything he possibly could to see that she had all she could ever want or need. Wasn't that what a husband was supposed to do? What more did she want from him?

He missed how things had been when they first got married, the time they spent together, just as much as she did, but it couldn't be helped. He had tried telling her time and again that everything he did, every minute he spent out on the rodeo circuit, was for her and the family they were hoping to have. Why couldn't she see that?

A sudden throbbing at his temple caused him to squeeze his eyelids shut and steady himself against the tiled wall of the shower. The image of Bria, tears running down her cheeks, appeared behind his closed eyes.

"I needed my husband with me when I lost the baby, Sam," she said, her voice filled with anguish. "I needed you to hold me and tell me that everything was going to be all right. But you weren't here. You're never here. You're always out on the road somewhere and I'm here alone."

Sam opened his eyes and felt as if he had taken a sucker punch to the gut. The snippet of memory was brief, but he knew as surely as he knew his own name that it was all too real. Bria had been pregnant and suffered a miscarriage.

His chest tightened and he had to stop for a minute to take a big gulp of air as a keen sense of loss for the baby they had both wanted so much coursed through him. He had fathered a child and no matter that it had been lost early in the pregnancy, he had cared deeply for the tiny life created from his and Bria's love for each other.

Sam tried desperately to remember what had happened, why she had lost the baby and exactly where he had been. But the more he tried to force himself to recall what had taken place, the more frustrated he became. For the life of him he couldn't remember when Bria had become pregnant or how far along she had been. Had it only been a few weeks ago or had she been pregnant when she bought the early home-pregnancy test?

He took a deep breath. It came as no surprise that he had been out on the road somewhere with the rodeo company when it happened. That was what he did, how he made their living. He thought she understood that.

As he continued to think about it, a heavy yoke of guilt settled across his shoulders, as well as the accompanying shame. He hadn't returned home right away and that was something he didn't think he could ever forgive himself for doing. His pride hadn't allowed him to be there for her when she needed him most. But he had to wait until he was certain he could face her without allowing her to see how the loss of their child had affected him. If he hadn't, she would have known immediately that she had married a weak, inept man who wasn't nearly as strong as she thought he was.

Turning off the spray of warm water, he grabbed a towel and quickly dried off. As he pulled on his boxer briefs and a pair of jeans, he wondered how he was going to let her know that he had remembered their loss without causing Bria any more emotional pain than she had already been through. It was no wonder she had been on edge and not quite herself lately. His run-in with that brindle bull had only added to the upset she had already been going through trying to come to terms with the miscarriage.

Walking into the bedroom, he sat on the bench at the end of the bed and reached for his boots, but stopped short when he realized how many times in the past few days he had made references to them trying to become pregnant. He cursed himself for his faulty memory and the pain he must have put Bria through each time he mentioned it.

Could that have been the real reason she made the remark about not feeling like his wife? Did she view his comments as purposely hurtful and insensitive?

Sam shook his head as he pulled on his boots. He didn't think that was the case. Bria was more reasonable than that. She knew he hadn't been able to remember about the baby and wouldn't have been so casual with his remarks about making her pregnant if he had. No, there was something else going on with her and he intended to find out what it was.

He stood up and, putting on a chambray shirt, began fastening the snaps as he walked out of the bedroom toward the stairs. But as he started down the steps, he paused to stare at the blank space where several pictures had always been. What had happened to them?

When he and Bria got married, the first thing she had done was designate it as the wall where all family photos were to be hung. He had been so tired the night before, he hadn't noticed them being gone, but he sure as hell noticed it now. Their wedding photo, along with pictures of his brothers and Bria's family, were conspicuously absent. What else had changed in the past several months? he wondered as he continued to the kitchen.

"Bria, what did you do with all the pictures on the wall by the stairs?"

"I took them down," she said without further explanation. Her back was to him, but he could tell by the set of her slender shoulders that she still wasn't happy with him.

Pulling out the chair at the head of the table, he sat down in front of the plate of food she had brought back to the kitchen. "When did you take them down?"

"It's been a while."

Sam frowned. Trying to get answers out of her was like trying to pull teeth. "Was there a reason?"

"I thought they would look better somewhere else." She poured him a fresh cup of coffee and brought it over to the table. "While you eat breakfast I'm going upstairs to make the bed. I'll be back in a few minutes."

As he watched her leave the room, he decided not to discuss what little bit of memory he had recovered about the baby. Bria wasn't in the best frame of mind and he didn't want to upset her further. Besides, if his memory was starting to return, maybe he would remember more details about what happened and have a better idea of how to approach the subject when they did talk.

He picked up his fork and started to take a bite of the scrambled eggs, but thinking about her accusations upstairs caused him to frown. Why didn't she think he needed her for more than making love?

His appetite suddenly deserting him, he placed the fork back on the plate and picked up his coffee mug. How did she want him to be dependent on her? Why would any woman want a man like that?

Sam shook his head. He wasn't sure, but hell would freeze over before he became a sorry excuse for a man like his biological father, Joe Rafferty, had been.

Staring over the rim of his cup, Sam rarely thought

about his life before he went to live on the Last Chance Ranch. He wasn't proud of where he came from or what he had done to survive after his mother died, and as Hank always said, the past was history and couldn't be changed, so it was best not to waste time mulling it over. But occasionally, when he did allow himself to think about his life before entering the foster care system, Sam couldn't help wondering how he and Nate would have turned out if the authorities hadn't stepped in after their irresponsible father abandoned them.

Of course, when their mother was alive, their lives hadn't been all that bad. They had been dirt poor, but Susan Rafferty had never let her sons know it. She had seen to it that they had everything they needed. They hadn't realized it at the time, but she had paid a high price for that. Working sometimes twelve hours a day, seven day a week, just to put food on the table and keep a roof over their heads, she had worked herself into an early grave while their father sat around making excuses why he had to quit his latest job and why he couldn't find another one.

"Sam, did you hear me?" Bria asked, bringing him out of his introspection and back to the present.

"Sorry, I wasn't paying attention." Lost in thought, he hadn't realized she had come back downstairs.

"I asked if you'd like to go for a walk down by the creek after you finish breakfast." She smiled. "I thought you might like to do some fishing while I read."

"That sounds pretty good," he said, nodding. "Anything is better than just sitting around." He was glad to see her mood had improved a little and that he was apparently out of the doghouse for the time being.

She pointed to his untouched plate. "Aren't you going to eat?"

"I told you upstairs what I wanted for breakfast," he said, grinning as he took a sip from the cup he held. "But since that's not on the menu, I think I'll just settle for this cup of coffee."

She nodded. "Very wise choice, Mr. Rafferty."

As they walked the short distance to the creek behind the barn, Bria watched to make sure Sam wasn't becoming overly tired. She could tell he was feeling a lot better, but there was still the possibility of him having a bit of vertigo and although he would never admit it, he tired easily.

Sighing, she thought about their earlier disagreement and chastised herself for bringing up things that they had argued about for the past couple of years with no resolution. There was really no point in revisiting them, because he couldn't seem to get what she was trying to tell him and probably never would. But she had been so frustrated with his stubbornness and refusal to admit that he might need her help, she had verbally lashed out before she could stop herself. That was something she couldn't let happen again. He had already questioned her several times since coming home from the hospital about what was going on and she wasn't sure how many more times she could keep her cool and dance around telling him.

She glanced up at his handsome profile. Sam certainly wasn't making it easy for her, either. There was obstinate and then there was Sam Rafferty obstinate. He managed to take pigheadedness to a whole new level and could no doubt push Job past his limit of patience.

That's why Sam hadn't realized, and she wasn't going to tell him, that after taking his breakfast to the kitchen, she had gone back upstairs to wait outside the bathroom until he finished his shower. Nor did he know that she had been standing in the hall just out of sight to make sure he navigated the stairs without problems. He might like to think that except for his memory he was almost back to normal, but she knew better. If the truth was known, he did, too. But he would never let on. It would be the ultimate sin for him to admit to any kind of weakness, even if it was a temporary condition.

"Why don't we sit down under the cottonwood tree," she asked, pulling a blanket from the picnic basket she had packed before they left the house. It was close enough to the creek for Sam to fish and provided a nice amount of shade to protect them from the early-summer sun.

"It looks like it's going to be a hot one today," he said, putting his fishing pole down to take the blanket from her. Spreading it out, he nodded toward the creek. "Any self-respecting catfish is going to be lying in a hole in the creek bed where it's cooler."

"You aren't even going to try?" she asked, setting the basket down. "I thought you liked to fish."

"I do. And I never said I wasn't going to try," he said, grinning. "I'm just warning you not to be sur-

prised when I cuss a blue streak, vow never to go fishing again, then give up and take a nap."

She laughed. "In other words, we won't be having
fish for supper tonight."

"It's highly unlikely, sweetheart," he said, lowering
himself to the edge of the blanket.

His easy grin and the teasing conversation caused a
longing inside Bria that she did her best to ignore. This
was a side of Sam she hadn't seen often enough in the
past couple of years and she had missed it.

Watching him bait the hook with some kind of
big, ugly bug, she rested her back against the tree and
opened her book. Getting lost in a good story was much
easier than allowing herself to get wrapped up in memories of what Sam used to be like or the fantasy that
there was a chance for them in the future. As soon as
the doctor released Sam to go back to work, whether
his memory had returned or not, she knew he would
revert to his workaholic ways, go back out on the road,
and she would end up spending the majority of her time
alone. She sighed. It was inevitable because he had already indicated that he intended to go back to work as
soon as possible and, as he put it, "everything would
go back to normal."

Thirty minutes later, when Sam put down his fishing
pole, took off his hat, then lay back to put his head in
her lap, Bria jumped. She had finally managed to become involved in the story she was reading and hadn't
realized he was giving up on trying to catch a fish.

"I didn't hear you start swearing or vow that you'll
never go fishing again," she said, cursing the breath-

less tone of her voice. Sam was gazing up at her with a smoldering light in his dark blue eyes—a look that never failed to send shivers of anticipation coursing through every part of her.

"I guess I'm getting mellow in my old age," he said, smiling as he reached up to lightly trace her jawline with his fingertips. "I decided to leave that old catfish alone today."

"And why is that?" she asked, returning his smile.

"I got to thinking that he might be lying in that hole in the creek bed with his lady and it would be a shame to take him away from that." He winked. "I know how I'd feel if somebody disturbed us."

His gentle touch and suggestive tone set off warning bells in the back of her mind. She couldn't fall back into the same old pattern. Nothing had changed between them. When Sam was home he had always been attentive and let her know in no uncertain terms that he desired her. The only problem was, that only happened a few days out of the month.

As far as she was concerned, that wasn't enough. Not when he had personnel who could travel with the livestock while he coordinated everything from the ranch. In the beginning, that had been his plan. But as the business became a success, it seemed to drive Sam to set new goals and strive to achieve more. And somewhere along the way he had lost sight of the hopes and dreams they'd had for their life, their marriage, their family.

"You're looking awfully serious all of a sudden," he said, taking the book from her hands to place it on the blanket beside her.

"Since we clearly aren't having fish, I was wondering what I'm going to make for supper," she said, grasping at the first thing that came to mind. "Would you like chicken or steak?"

"I'm a born-and-bred Texan, sweetheart," he said, laughing. "What do you think?"

She hoped her smile looked less forced than it felt. "Steak it is."

"I've got an idea," he said, looking thoughtful. "Why don't we drive over to Beaver Dam this evening and have dinner at the Broken Spoke Roadhouse."

At first Bria wasn't sure that was a good idea. He knew several of the ranchers over that way. What if someone in the tiny town had heard about their separation and impending divorce and made a comment in front of Sam?

But she abandoned that possibility almost immediately. Sam was a very private man and wouldn't have mentioned it to anyone unless he had to. To her knowledge, the only people who knew about the end of their marriage were his brothers and her sister. Mariah lived all the way up in Amarillo and didn't know a soul in Beaver Dam, and his brothers were five of the most honorable men she had ever met. They would all rather die than betray Sam's trust.

"That sounds nice," she finally said, warming to the idea. "Are you sure you feel up to it?"

He looked exasperated. "I told you—"

"I know." She sighed. "Other than your memory, you're just fine."

"Yup." He yawned and, reaching for his wide-brimmed hat, covered his eyes with it. "I think I'll take a little nap before we have lunch and start back to the house to get ready for our big night out."

While Sam slept, Bria tried to get back into the story of a pioneer woman on the wild frontier. As long as she was lost in the woman's journey and the trials she faced, Bria didn't have to think about the man with his head in her lap sleeping as if he didn't have a care in the world. The man who was putting her through the biggest trial she had faced in all of her twenty-eight years and didn't even realize it.

Four

As Sam put his hand to the small of Bria's back to guide her to a table in the back of the Broken Spoke Roadhouse, he noticed several cowboys turn to give her an appreciative glance. There was no doubt she was the best-looking woman in the entire joint and probably better looking than most of the men had ever been privileged to see.

Deep in the heart of ranch country, the Broken Spoke was a typical Western watering hole with chipped Formica tables, chrome chairs with cracked vinyl upholstery and country music blaring on the jukebox. The lighting was a little too dim and the music was a bit too loud, but it was clean, and catering to the ranchers and their hired hands who called the area home, the bar and grill served the best steaks in three counties. Not even the steaks he had eaten in five-star restaurants could compare. It was usually packed with the men outnumbering women four to one. Tonight was no different.

"Maybe this wasn't such a good idea," Sam said, frowning as he scanned the room.

Bria gave him a questioning look. "But I thought you liked the food here."

"I do. But I forgot that half the joint's clientele are looking to get lucky."

"What about the other half?" she asked, sitting in the chair he held for her.

"They're either too old or too backward to do anything but leer."

He glared at a fresh-faced, red-haired cowboy who stared a little longer than Sam thought was polite. Apparently seeing the wisdom in turning his gaze elsewhere, the kid went back to giving his full attention to the plate of food in front of him.

"I see they've added a small dance floor since we were here the last time," Bria said, pointing to the opposite side of the room close to the jukebox.

"We'll have to dance a slow one or two before we leave," Sam said, smiling. If there was anything Bria loved to do more than dance, he didn't know of it.

"That might not be a good idea." She looked worried. "You've had a big day already and I don't want you to overdo it."

He blew out a frustrated breath. "I haven't had a dizzy spell in a while and you haven't let me do anything but lie around since coming home from the hospital."

"That was only yesterday," she said, her expression disapproving.

"I'm not used to doing nothing, Bria."

Why couldn't she understand his need to stay busy and be productive? As Hank always told him and his brothers, having nothing to do was the fastest way to get into a whole heap of trouble. Since cleaning up his act at the age of fifteen, he had made sure to stay busy in more productive ways and avoided being idle for too long.

Bria gazed at him a moment before shaking her head. "Please, Sam, can we discuss all this later? I really don't want to spoil the evening by arguing with you right now."

Covering her hand with his, he smiled. "That sounds good to me, sweetheart. But take my word for it, one or two slow dances with you after we eat is not going to hurt me."

As he lightly stroked her fingers with his thumb, he realized something wasn't right. Moving his hand to glance down at hers resting on the table, he immediately noticed that her wedding and engagement rings were missing. The only time he knew of her taking them off was to shower or the few odd times when she did dishes instead of using the dishwasher. Where were they?

"Why aren't you wearing your rings?" he asked, tracing the third finger on her left hand.

He watched her nibble on her lower lip as if trying to decide what to say. "I…left them at the house."

"Why?"

"I forgot…to put them back on," she answered, not quite meeting his curious gaze.

Her hesitant tone made him wonder if she thought he might be angry that she wasn't wearing them. But that didn't make any sense. He wasn't the controlling type and had never indicated that he wanted her to wear them unless *she* wanted to. Hell, he rarely wore his wedding band. Working around livestock all the time, there was too big of a chance to get a ring caught on something and break a finger, or worse, lose one.

"It's all right, Bria. It's really no big deal." He smiled. "We're both just as married whether we have on our wedding rings or not."

Nodding, she picked up one of the paper menus. "I don't suppose I have to ask what you're having."

"Nope." Leaning back in the chair, he grinned. "I'll be having my usual sixteen-ounce porterhouse with a side of coleslaw, baked beans and fries."

"How imaginative of you," she said, laughing.

"Hey, I'm nothing if not predictable." Her light laughter sounded like music to his ears. She hadn't done a lot of that in the past couple of days and he had missed the delightful sound.

Forty-five minutes later, as they finished the slices of pecan pie he had ordered for desert, someone fed coins into the jukebox and selected a popular country love song. "Would you like to dance, sweetheart?" Sam asked when he noticed Bria watching the two couples on the dance floor slowly swaying in time to the music.

She glanced from him to the dance floor then back. "Only if you promise to tell me if you start feeling lightheaded or get tired."

Rising to his feet, he held out his hand. "I give you my word, you'll be the first to know if that happens."

When she smiled and placed her soft palm against his, Sam's heart stalled. His wife was without a shadow of a doubt the sexiest, most desirable woman he had ever had the pleasure to know and he counted himself one of the luckiest son of a guns on the face of the earth that she was his.

As he led her out onto the floor, he noticed several of the cowboys in the joint stopped what they were doing to watch. He couldn't blame them. Bria looked absolutely amazing. Her designer jeans were made to look as if they had been well-worn and had a couple of stylish holes in the thighs, exposing an enticing glimpse of her smooth skin, and the formfitting black tank top with a design made of the finest Austrian crystals on the front hugged her breasts and the feminine indention of her waist like a lover's caress.

His lower belly tightened, but when he wrapped his arms around her and she lifted hers to encircle his shoulders, he wasn't the least bit surprised to find himself hard as hell in less time than it took to draw his next breath. Gazing into her luminous emerald eyes, he pulled her closer and knew the moment she felt the hard ridge of his arousal pressed to her soft stomach.

"Sam, maybe we should sit down," she said, starting to pull away from him. "You might become dizzy."

He held her snug against him. "Sweetheart, I'm fine. That's just a myth."

She looked confused. "What do you mean?"

He chuckled as he whispered close to her ear. "There

really is enough blood in a man's body to support both—"

"I get it," she interrupted, her cheeks turning a pretty pink. "I didn't mean *that*."

"What did you mean?" he asked, kissing the tip of her nose.

"I thought you might not want everyone to know that you're…um, feeling amorous," she whispered.

He looked around. "The lighting in here is so bad, I doubt that will be a problem." Tilting his hat back, he grinned as he rested his forehead against hers. "But it doesn't matter. The last I heard, it's perfectly acceptable for a man to become aroused when he's holding his wife. Especially when she's the hottest woman in the whole damn state."

"I'm a little tired," she said, suddenly pushing away from him. "I think it would be best if we leave."

"All right." Confused by the urgency he heard in her voice, Sam followed her back to their table, tossed some money on the top of it for their meal, along with a generous tip, then taking her hand in his, led her to the exit. Once they were standing in the parking lot, he held out his hand for the keys to the SUV. "You're tired. I'll drive home."

"We've been over this before, Sam," she said, sounding as if her patience was wearing thin. "Get used to it. You're not driving until the doctor releases you to do so. Now, get in the truck or I swear I'll leave you standing here in this parking lot."

Something was definitely going on with her, but Sam decided not to push her to tell him what it was and instead got into the passenger side of the SUV. Bria looked as if she could either tear his head off or burst into tears and he didn't have a clue why.

But one thing was certain. He was for damn sure going to find out when they got back to the ranch.

As Bria drove the twenty miles back to Sugar Creek Ranch, neither she nor Sam had a lot to say. She knew she had acted irrationally, but her nerves were getting the better of her. For the past twenty-four hours she had been under a tremendous amount of stress, pretending that nothing was wrong, that they were still happily married. Unfortunately, Sam didn't remember that wasn't the case and seemed to be launching a sensual assault that was threatening to drive her to the brink of insanity.

Then there was the matter of hiding the truth about their relationship without lying to him. When he had asked her about her wedding and engagement rings, she had told him the truth. Three months ago when she moved out of the house, she had taken them off and left them in a small black velvet box on top of the dresser. She had forgotten to find them and put them back on. But she'd had so much on her mind, trying to make sure Sam didn't overdo things, pretending that everything was all right between them when it wasn't, that it was nothing short of a miracle she could remember her own name, let alone her rings.

When she drove up to the side of the ranch house and parked the SUV, she was surprised when he didn't immediately open the door to get out. "Is something wrong, Sam?" she asked, hoping the vertigo hadn't returned.

"You tell me, Bria," he answered, turning to look at her. His eyes held hers and until that moment, she hadn't really understood what it meant to feel as if someone's piercing gaze went all the way to her soul. She did now.

She caught her breath. Had he remembered something? Maybe a fragment about their marriage being in trouble?

"I don't know what you mean, Sam."

"There used to be a time when you loved for me to let you feel how much I want you. Loved for me to show you what you did to me and how much you tied me in knots." He shook his head. "Now you get jumpy as hell if I get within ten feet of you, and try to put as much distance between us as you possibly can."

She should have known that he would start questioning why she kept sidestepping his advances. "Sam, I—"

"Is there someone else?" he interrupted, his tone holding a hard edge that she had never heard before. "If there is, I can tell you right now the son of a bitch is in for the fight of his miserable life."

"No, Sam, there's never been anyone but you," she said honestly. "You're the only man I've ever wanted to be with."

He must have heard the truth in her words, because his tone softened. "Then what's the problem, sweetheart? You know you can tell me anything."

Bria closed her eyes for a moment as she fought the urge to throw herself into his arms, to have him hold her and her hold him until all their problems melted away.

But that was something she simply couldn't allow herself to do. It had never worked before and she knew it wouldn't work now. His accident hadn't been the solution to what was wrong in their relationship, it had only added another complication.

"I guess I'm just letting my nerves get the better of me," she finally managed to say.

She wasn't lying. Her nerves had been stretched to the breaking point ever since she watched the bull run him down, and they hadn't gotten any better since coming back to the ranch. Having to watch every single thing she said to him was like walking a tightrope with no safety net.

"I'm sorry you've had so much to deal with lately." Leaning across the console, he gave her a kiss so tender it brought tears to her eyes. "When we go upstairs to bed, I'm going to hold you until all that worry melts away and you feel secure again."

"I don't think…that would be a good idea," she said haltingly.

"I do." He sounded so sure, it was hard for her not to believe that it was all that simple.

The feel of his gentle kiss and his heartfelt pledge to make her feel safe caused her chest to tighten. Why hadn't he been there to tell her something like this when she had lost their baby? She had needed his strength and comfort then more than she ever needed anything in her life and he had been somewhere out on the West Coast, playing nursemaid to a herd of rodeo livestock.

Unfortunately, she couldn't confront him about it now. She couldn't tell him how desolate she had felt without him with her or how emotionally hurt she had been when he did come home and wouldn't talk to her about their loss. Besides, they had already had that conversation and like everything else that had taken place the past six months, he didn't remember it.

But what excuse was she going to use to keep from going to bed with him? Tonight he wasn't as exhausted as he had been the evening before. There was no way he would turn in for the night without her with him. What could she possibly say to explain sleeping in the bedroom down the hall?

As she tried to think of something—anything—to keep from telling him about their pending divorce, Sam got out and came around to open the driver's door to help her from the SUV. "Come on, sweetheart. Let's go upstairs so that I can hold you and make you forget about all the things that are bothering you."

Thirty minutes later as she finished getting ready for bed, Bria spent as much time as she could changing into her nightshirt and brushing her teeth. Once she opened the bathroom door, Sam would be waiting to take her into his arms and unknowingly add to her tension, rather than help alleviate it.

"Is everything all right in there?" Sam asked from the other side of the door.

She knew she couldn't stall any longer. She would just have to wait until he went to sleep, then try to get out of bed without waking him and go down the hall to the guest bedroom.

Taking a deep breath, she opened the door. "I was brushing my—" She stopped short at the sight of Sam standing in front of her wearing nothing but a big smile. "Aren't you going to wear something to sleep in?"

His smile turned to a grin. "You know I'm not a big fan of wearing anything to bed."

"You wore your underwear last night," she said, knowing he had been too tired to take them off.

Maybe that was the key to her dilemma. Maybe if Sam was so exhausted each night that he fell asleep as soon as he got into bed he wouldn't question her sleeping in a separate room…

She immediately abandoned that idea. There was only one way she knew that would exhaust a man with seemingly boundless energy, and making love with him was definitely not an option.

"You look like you're ready to drop in your tracks." His deep baritone sent a shiver of excitement straight up her spine.

More like melt into a puddle at his feet, she thought as she stared at his magnificent physique. Well over six feet tall, Sam had the body of an athlete—lean, with well-defined muscles and not an ounce of spare flesh. When her gaze drifted lower, it took everything in her not to moan. Even relaxed, he was impressive, and she had missed being with him so very much.

"Come here," he said, reaching for her.

The moment he pulled her to his broad, bare chest, a delicious tingling sensation raced straight up Bria's spine and sent heat flowing through her veins. She had always loved Sam's body, loved the contrast between them and the feel of her smoother skin pressed to his hair-roughened flesh. And it appeared that fascination hadn't changed.

If anything, the awareness of the differences in their bodies was more acute than ever. Feeling the ridges of bulging muscle made hard by years of ranch work pressed to her from shoulders to knees caused her breath to come out on a soft sigh and a delightful tightening in the most feminine part of her. The sensations were a swift reminder of just how long it had been since Sam had held her, loved her.

"You're shivering," he said, lightly skimming his palms from her shoulders down her arms to catch her hands in his. "I didn't realize how much tension and stress the accident caused you, sweetheart."

At that moment, it wasn't his being pummeled by the bull that was causing her to tremble. It was his raw masculinity and the temptation he posed that had put her on sensory overload.

"I may be…coming down with a cold," she said, hoping her excuse didn't sound as lame to him as it did to her. "Maybe I should sleep in one of the guest rooms. If I do have something contagious, I don't think it would be a good idea for you to get whatever it is."

He shook his head and led her over to the bed. "If you're getting sick, that's all the more reason for you to be in bed with me so that I can take care of you."

His statement was like waving a red flag in front of a bull and helped shatter the sensual spell he had been casting over her. "Sam, that doesn't make sense." She pulled away from him. "Why is it perfectly acceptable for you to take care of me when I'm not feeling well, but it's unheard of for me to help you?"

"Because I'm your husband," he said, frowning. "The day I married you, I promised to take care of you."

"And wives are supposed to do the same thing for their husbands," she retorted. She could tell by the stubborn set of his lean jaw that, as usual, he wasn't getting what she was trying to tell him. "I repeated the same wedding vows you did, Sam."

"Bria, sweetheart, you're getting too upset and not making a lot of sense."

"I pledged to be with you in sickness as well as in health," she went on. She pointed to his head and the now-fading bruise along his cheek. "You having post-concussion syndrome certainly qualifies as the 'in sickness' part of those vows. But from the moment you came home from the hospital you've insisted that there's nothing wrong and won't let me do things to help you. How am I supposed to keep my promise if you won't let me?"

"Does this have something to do with your monthly—"

"Oh, good grief! This has nothing at all to do with my cycle," she said, cutting him off. "Why do men think that every time a woman disagrees with him or becomes upset, she has to be experiencing PMS or some other hormonal imbalance?"

He looked mystified by her outburst. "Are you sure? You do get a little cranky sometimes."

She wanted to find something and smack him with it. "If you'll remember, we've had this argument before and you're not listening any more now than you were when I—" she stopped herself just in time "—then." She had started to say before she left him, but he didn't remember any of that, and telling him now wasn't going to accomplish anything and might just make things more difficult in the long run.

"Bria, you know I can't do that," he said, his frustration causing lines to etch his forehead. "I don't remember anything since the first part of the year. If there's something I need to know or that you want to tell me, I'm listening."

A sudden feeling of utter defeat settled over her. There was so much she wanted to tell him about needing him to rely on her as much as she did him, about how she wanted to feel as if she was an equal partner in their marriage. She wanted to ask him why he had waited to come home after she lost their child, and when he did, why he'd acted as if the pregnancy had never existed. But he couldn't remember her pregnancy, much less the last time she had confronted him with all her questions, so there was really no point in repeating herself.

"Go to bed, Sam," she said tiredly. It really wasn't his fault he couldn't recall anything, but it didn't make it any less upsetting for her. "Maybe you'll understand once you've regained your memory."

When she turned and started toward the door, she might have escaped had he not put his hand on her arm. "Stay in here with me, Bria. It's where you belong."

His touch and the sincerity in his voice were her undoing. She didn't have the energy or the will left to protest.

"We can't—"

"I know, sweetheart," he said gently. "I'm just going to hold you."

Lying down on what was once her side of the bed, she held her breath when Sam stretched out beside her and gathered her to him. The feel of his strong arms holding her so securely against him, the steady beat of his heart beneath her palm where it rested on his chest and his clean masculine scent caused her to blink back tears. She was back in his arms for the first time in months and it felt as if she had come home. The only problem was, as soon as he regained his memory and their divorce became final, she would no longer have the right to be there.

When he woke up the next morning, Sam wasn't overly surprised to find that Bria was already up and had most likely gone downstairs to make breakfast. Hopefully, she would be more rested and in a better mood than last night.

Staring at the ceiling, he thought about what she had said just before they had gone to bed. What made her think he didn't need her?

Just because he insisted on doing things for himself didn't mean she wasn't a vital part of his life. Why couldn't she see that he worked hard and had bent over backward to make things easier for her? That it was important to him that he provide her with a nice house to live in and nice things to wear? Or that by gritting his teeth and not allowing her to see his weaknesses, he was actually putting her needs before his own and showing her how much he cherished her? Didn't she realize how amazing he thought she was? How honored he was to be her husband?

Unlike what his father had done for his mother, Sam intended to see that Bria wasn't saddled with a man who was too lazy to do anything for himself. Of course, she didn't know anything about his life before he and Nate were put into foster care, didn't have a clue what had sent them to the Last Chance Ranch or how it drove him to be a better man now. And that was just the way Sam wanted it to stay. The few times she asked him about his childhood, he had told her that she didn't want to know and found a way to divert her attention.

He wasn't proud of his past, didn't want to talk about it and didn't want Bria to think less of him for where he came from and the mistakes he had made in his youth. Hank Calvert had assured his foster sons that no one had to know about what they had done to land themselves in his care. It was how they acted and what they did moving forward that counted.

A sudden dull ache seemed to wrap around his skull and, groaning, Sam closed his eyes against the pain squeezing his brain.

"Sam, I've tried to tell you what's wrong with our marriage, what's wrong with us," Bria said tearfully as she put stacks of her clothes into a suitcase. "But you won't listen and I can't live like this anymore." She stopped packing to turn and face him. "Husbands and wives are supposed to communicate and tell each other what's wrong, then work out a solution together. But your idea of 'fixing things' is to ignore whatever

problems we have and hope they'll miraculously go away. Maybe I could understand you better if I knew why you're so self-contained, but I don't know anything about your life before you went to live with Hank Calvert. Husbands usually share something like that with their wives, but you won't even give me that much. It's almost as if you didn't exist before you went to live at the Last Chance Ranch."

As the pressure in his head eased, Sam's heart thumped against his ribs like a war drum. Opening his eyes, he threw back the covers and sat up on the side of the bed. Had Bria actually left him? She was here now. But what the hell had happened and how had they resolved the situation?

Rubbing his temples, he desperately tried to remember what had taken place and where Bria had been going. But as had been the case each time he recovered a scrap of his memory, the events surrounding it were elusive and just out of reach.

He stood up and headed for the shower. Lying in bed was not going to get him the answers he needed. And whether he liked what he learned or not, he had to know.

After a quick shower, Sam got dressed and started downstairs. He had no idea what he was going to do in order to figure things out, but questioning Bria wasn't on the table. For one thing, he didn't remember enough about what took place to know how to approach the matter. And for another, not revealing the fact that his memory was returning might buy him the time he needed to know how to deal with the situation when it did come back.

He was halfway to the bottom step when he stopped dead in his tracks and slowly turned his head toward the wall where the family pictures hung. Bria had told him that she had taken them down to put them elsewhere. But if she had hung them up in another room, he hadn't found them.

As he continued to the kitchen, he thought about her missing wedding and engagement rings and her reaction when he had asked about them. She had mentioned forgetting to put them on, but she hadn't been able to look him in the eye and quickly changed the subject.

A knot began to form in his gut and by the time he sat down at the big round oak table in the kitchen, his appetite was nonexistent. He needed to check out the house to see what else was missing. Unless he was mistaken, Bria didn't live at Sugar Creek Ranch anymore. Was she only there to see him through the recovery from his accident?

"Good morning, Sam," Bria said, turning from the stove to face him. "I've got bacon and hash browns ready. Would you like pancakes or eggs for breakfast?"

"Whatever is easiest," he said, distracted by his disturbing thoughts. How was he going to search the house to see what else had changed or was missing without her realizing what he was up to?

"One is about as easy as the other," she said, smiling.

"A couple of fried eggs would be fine." He waited until she had turned back to the stove to tend to the eggs before asking, "What do you have planned for the day?"

"I thought if you're feeling up to it, we could drive up to Stephenville to pick up what I'll need for Jaron's birthday dinner." She placed the eggs, bacon and hash browns on a plate, then walked over to the table to set it in front of him. "But if you'd rather just take it easy, Mariah and your brothers will be here tomorrow. She and I can go shopping for what I need while you visit with the guys."

"If it's all the same to you, I was thinking about going over the ranch books to see if I can figure out what's been going on the past several months," he said, looking down at the food on his plate. With his appetite gone, the food looked about as appealing as a piece of wagon harness.

"You hate doing paperwork," she said, frowning as she sank into one of the straight-backed chairs.

"Who knows? It might help me remember something." He shrugged one shoulder. "But don't think you have to wait to go shopping on my account. I'll be in the office most of the day going over the books."

"I don't want to leave you alone," she said, shaking her head. "Mariah and I can go tomorrow."

"I won't be alone." He forced a smile he wasn't feeling. "T.J. called yesterday to tell me he's driving up a day early and should be here by midmorning."

Bria frowned. "I don't remember anyone calling yesterday."

"You were in the shower getting ready to go to the Broken Spoke." He picked up his fork to push the hash browns around his plate. "I guess I just forgot to tell you."

"How can he possibly be here by midmorning?" she asked, looking doubtful. "It's an eight-hour drive from Tranquility to get here."

"He's just north of Round Rock buying a new quarter horse stallion he wants to improve his herd." He reached over to cover her hand resting on the table with his and noticed her rings were still missing. It made him more determined than ever to see what else had changed around the house. "You go ahead and make plans to get your shopping out of the way today. That will give you and Mariah more time to catch up when she gets here."

"Actually, that does sound like a good plan," she finally said, nodding. "It would be nice to get some of the cooking done tomorrow instead of having it all to do on Sunday."

"And you don't have to wait until T.J. gets here," he added. "I give you my word that I won't be doing anything more strenuous than pushing a pencil and using a calculator. And if I do get tired, I'll take a nap."

She shook her head. "I don't think leaving you alone just yet would be wise. I'll wait until T.J. gets here before I leave."

"I promise I'll be fine, sweetheart," he assured her, then patted the device clipped to his belt. "And if I need something, I always have my cell phone."

"No. If something happens before T.J. gets here, I'd never forgive myself," she said, shaking her head.

An hour later, as he and T.J. watched Bria's SUV drive down the ranch road leading to the main highway,

Sam got up from the porch swing. "I'm going inside for a can of soda. You want a beer?"

"Sure," T.J. said. "You're not having one?"

"Nope." Sam grinned. "If Bria smells it on my breath when she gets home, you and I will both be in big trouble."

"Aw, hell, no," T.J. said, laughing. "The last thing I need is Bria on the warpath with me. I've had enough tongue-lashing lately from an irate woman. I don't need another one."

"Still battling with your neighbor?" Sam asked, laughing at T.J.'s exasperated expression.

"Don't get me started," his brother said, groaning. "The less I have to think about that woman, the better."

"I'll be back out in a minute with your beer," Sam said, grinning.

As he entered the house, he had a few things to check to see if they were missing before he got their drinks and rejoined T.J. on the porch. If they were missing, then he would know for certain that Bria was there only because of his injury and the advice from the doctor about letting him recover his memory on his own without putting him under any kind of stress.

Starting in the dining room, he walked straight to the sideboard and opened the cabinet beneath one of the drawers. His heart slammed against his ribs and the painful knot that formed in his gut damn near knocked him to his knees as the ugly truth began to sink in. He didn't need to take his search any farther. The absence of her grandmother's antique fruit bowl and the silver platter that had been in her family for three generations were all the confirmation he needed.

He struggled to draw his next breath. His fears had been confirmed. Bria no longer lived at Sugar Creek Ranch.

Five

"Bria, do you want me to start making the pie crusts?"

Looking up from the apples she had been peeling, Bria laughed at the sight of her sister. "How on earth did you get flour in your hair?"

"The stupid bag exploded when I opened it," Mariah said, making a face. She used the back of her hand to brush back a strand of dark brown hair that had escaped her ponytail. "I think I must have been squeezing the bag when I cut the top off."

"Why didn't you just use what was in the canister?" Bria asked, turning her attention back to the apples in the bowl in front of her.

"Because that would have made more sense," Mariah said, laughing. "You know I don't have the first clue what I'm doing in the kitchen."

"Well, pie crust can be kind of tricky," Bria said

diplomatically. She put down the knife, then wiped her hands on a towel. "Why don't I make the crust while you finish peeling the apples."

Looking relieved, Mariah nodded. "I think that's an excellent idea." She picked up the paring knife Bria had been using. "But could you do me a favor?"

"What's that?" Bria asked, measuring cups of flour. When her sister hesitated, she looked up to see Mariah wearing a sheepish expression.

"Could you talk me through making the pies?"

Mariah had never shown the slightest interest in cooking and Bria was impressed that her sister had even offered to help. She suspected that the only reason Mariah had made the gesture this time was due to the fact that the dinner was for Jaron's birthday.

Grinning, Bria nodded. "You're going to try the old 'the way to a man's heart is through his stomach' tactic, huh?"

Her sister's cheeks turned bright pink. "I…uh, well… kind of. Jaron would rather have your apple pie than a birthday cake and I'd like to see if I can make one. I promise I'll do everything you tell me to and—"

"Of course I'll help you," Bria said, putting her arm around her younger sister's shoulders for a quick hug.

"Thanks, Bria," her sister said, hugging her back. "You're the best sister ever."

The moment she met him, Mariah had developed a huge crush on Jaron Lambert. Unfortunately, she had only been eighteen at the time and even now at twenty-three, Jaron still considered the ten years' difference in their ages insurmountable. Bria hoped that one day her sister could eventually see that and move on to find someone else.

By the time she had talked Mariah through making four apple pies for baking the next day, Bria was ready for a break. "Let's get ourselves a glass of iced tea and go out to sit on the porch swing for a few minutes," she suggested.

"Where did Sam and T.J. go?" Mariah asked as they walked out of the kitchen.

"Sam said they were going to check on one of the bulls over in the south pasture, but I'm pretty sure it's just an excuse to get out of the house for a while." Bria shrugged as she sat down on the swing. "You have no idea how difficult it's been to get him to take it easy."

"T.J. won't let him overdo things, will he?" Mariah asked, concerned.

Bria took a sip of her iced tea, then shook her head. "I don't think there's any way to stop Sam if he really wants to do something. But at least if anything happens it will be on T.J.'s shoulders and not mine."

Having Sam's foster brother arrive a couple of days early had been a godsend. T.J.'s visit had given her the break she needed from the stress she'd been under since Sam's release from the hospital, and it couldn't have come at a better time. Bria wasn't sure how much longer she would have been able to keep up the charade without cracking under the pressure of pretending everything was all right when it wasn't.

"Has Sam remembered anything at all?"

Bria sighed. "If he has, he hasn't mentioned it."

"Maybe having all his brothers around will help him

recall something," Mariah suggested. "The last time we had a get-together like this was just before you…"

When her sister's voice trailed off, Bria knew Mariah hated bringing up something that had been so emotionally painful for her. "Just before I miscarried."

Mariah nodded.

"It's all right. It was pretty rough for a while, but I can talk about it now without dissolving into tears," Bria assured her.

"When is Rosa coming back from visiting her sister?" Mariah asked, changing the subject. Bria suspected Mariah was afraid of upsetting her if they talked too much about the miscarriage.

"She isn't supposed to be back for another week, but I'm going to call her and give her another week off with pay," Bria answered. "She's as nice as can be, but I'm afraid she'll accidentally say something in front of Sam that he's not ready to hear."

Mariah shook her head. "You definitely don't want that."

"No, that's the last thing I need." Bria smiled. "With her on vacation, I suppose it's a good thing I like to cook."

"That's something I just can't understand." Mariah made a face. "I can think of all kinds of things I'd rather do than to stand at a stove to fix a meal."

Bria laughed. "But you wanted to make the apple pies."

"That's different." Mariah grinned. "I think you know why."

"Yes, I think I do," Bria said, grinning back.

They were quiet for several minutes before Mariah asked, "When do you think Jaron will be here?"

Smiling, Bria checked her watch. "He called Sam early this morning to tell us he was on his way, so I'd say just about any time now."

"Really?" A look of panic crossed Mariah's young face when Bria nodded. "Why didn't you tell me, Bria? I've been sitting here all this time and I'm a mess. I've got flour in my hair and—"

"You look adorable," she said, laughing. "The flour in your hair and the streak of cinnamon on your shirt will give credence to your having made the pies."

Mariah rolled her eyes as she stood up and started toward the door. "I associate the word *adorable* with puppies and kittens. I'd much rather look sexy and alluring. I'm going upstairs to take a shower and change clothes."

After her sister went inside, Bria sat for some time thinking about their conversation. Hopefully Mariah was right and having his brothers here for the weekend would help Sam start recalling things that had happened in recent months. If not, Bria wasn't sure how much longer she would be able to stay with him. Aside from the fact that she was supposed to start a new job in a couple of weeks, the more time she spent with Sam, the more it reminded her of how much she still cared for him and how dangerous that was to her peace of mind.

There was no doubt she would always love Sam. Unfortunately, sometimes loving someone wasn't enough. He hadn't been willing to help her work through the problems in their marriage and she couldn't go on with the way things had been.

Sighing, she rose from the swing to go back inside to start cutting up vegetables for a casserole. Leaving Sam had been one of the most difficult decisions she'd ever had to make and she would probably still be trying to make their marriage work if not for his extended absence when she miscarried. But being with him now was heaven and hell rolled into one and would only make it harder for her the second time she had to go. This time, she had been treated to a glimpse of what life would be like if he did stop traveling so much, and the more she saw of that life, the more she wanted it. The only problem was, he couldn't give that to her and she refused to settle for less.

As Sam sat at the head of the table in the formal dining room watching Bria interact with her sister and his brothers, a desperation like nothing he had ever known clawed at his insides. Since discovering that she was only at the ranch to help him recover from his accident, he hadn't been able to think of anything but how he was going to get her to stay. The only problem was, he didn't remember any of the details surrounding her leaving him and had no clue as to what he could do to make things right between them.

But even if he had recalled what had taken place, with all his brothers and her sister around the past couple of days, he wouldn't have been able to do anything about it. The only time they had been alone was when they had gone to bed at night.

"Earth to Sam. How are things out there in outer space, rocketman?" his brother asked, laughing.

Frowning, Sam looked at Nate. "What?"

"I asked you when you see the neurologist again," Nate answered, his tone sounding a bit short on patience.

"This coming Thursday." He needed to pay attention to what was going on. The last time he had let his mind wander, he had ended up being broadsided by a ton of hamburger on the hoof.

Without warning, a clear image of the bull coming toward him entered his mind and it took a moment for Sam to realize he was starting to remember things without the accompaniment of a dull headache or the sickening dizziness. Things were starting to come back to him a little faster now, and although he was positive he wasn't going to like what he recalled, he hoped to gain some insight into how to handle the situation with Bria.

"Have you all decided who's going to take Sam to the appointment?" he heard Bria ask as she and Mariah got up to cut pieces of apple pie for everyone.

"You're not going with me?" he asked, frowning. Her question had him abandoning his disturbing introspection in no time flat.

An uneasy silence suddenly blanketed the room and, glancing from one brother to the other, Sam noticed they all seemed to be taking an inordinate interest in the slices of pie being placed in front of them by Bria's sister.

Shaking her head, Bria walked over with his piece of pie. "Your brothers got together and decided I could use a day off to relax." She gave him a smile that sent his temperature up a good ten notches. "I might go to a spa or have my hair and nails done."

Even though he knew his brothers thought the world of Bria, Sam had never known them to be *that* considerate. But there was really nothing he could say that wouldn't tip them off that he was regaining his memory and he wasn't ready just yet to reveal that bit of information.

"It sounds nice, sweetheart," he said, picking up his fork. Her not being with him didn't sound nice at all, but at the moment there was nothing he could do but go along with their plan. Looking around the table at the five men shoveling pie into their mouths, he asked, "So which one of you drew the short straw and will be going with me?"

"Ah, hell, I'll bite the bullet and go down to Waco with you," Nate spoke up, grinning. "I met a cute little nurse while you were in the hospital down there. I wouldn't mind seeing her again."

"You're worse than a sailor with a woman in every port, Nate," Lane said, grinning as he shook his head. "I'll give you five-to-one odds in favor of all that carousing catching up to you one of these days."

With Lane's teasing remark, the celebratory mood had been successfully restored, and by the time they all polished off their slices of apple pie, it seemed like any other birthday dinner Bria had held for his brothers.

"Why don't we do something a little different this time," Sam said when he noticed how tired Bria looked. "The women did all the cooking and the least we can do is let them take it easy while we clean up and start the dishwasher."

Bria looked pleasantly surprised and Sam gave himself a mental pat on the back for thinking of it. "I'm not going to stop you if that's what you really want to do," she said, smiling.

"Sounds fair to me," Ryder said, nodding as he rose to his feet to take his plate into the kitchen. "Thanks to both of you lovely ladies for a great meal."

"Thank you," Lane said, picking up his glass and plate. "It's the best dinner I've had since the last birthday get-together."

Standing up, Nate went around the table to give Bria and Mariah a kiss on the cheek. "You girls are the best." He picked up his plate and as he walked through the door leading into the kitchen, called out, "Dibs on loading the dishwasher."

"Y'all outdid yourselves with dinner, ladies," T.J. added, following his brothers.

"They sure did," Jaron agreed. When he passed Mariah on his way to join the rest of the men in the kitchen, he stopped to give her a rare smile. "Thanks for making the pies, Mariah. Your apple pie is every bit as good as Bria's."

Sam watched the surprise on Mariah's face turn to a beaming smile. "There are still two whole pies left, in case you'd like another slice later," she said softly.

"I might just take you up on that," Jaron answered, continuing into the other room.

As Sam passed Bria on his way to join his brothers in the kitchen, he leaned down to kiss her soft lips.

"Thank you, sweetheart. I don't tell you often enough, but I appreciate everything you do for me and my brothers. Why don't you and Mariah find a place to put your feet up."

From the expression on her pretty face, he had clearly surprised her once again. "I love doing things like this for family, but are you sure you feel up to the cleaning detail?" she asked, looking a bit hesitant.

He nodded. "I'll be fine. Now, go and relax for a little while. You both deserve it."

"I think we might walk down by the creek for some girl talk," she said, smiling as she rose to her feet.

"Have a nice visit," he said, meaning it.

Entering the kitchen, Sam thought about how much he liked doing things to make Bria's life easier and about how good it made him feel. He frowned as he placed his dish on the counter. Was that what Bria meant by needing him to let her do things for him? Did it make her feel good to fuss over him?

"What's wrong now, Sam?" Nate asked, taking his plate to hand to Ryder to be rinsed off. "You aren't regretting your suggestion that we become busboys, are you?"

"Not in the least," Sam retorted, deciding to wait until he was alone to give his revelation more thought. "I just figured if we want more dinners like that, we'd better do something nice once in a while."

They all agreed and as they joked and laughed their way through cleaning the kitchen, Sam realized how much he had missed the easy camaraderie with the men he had grown up with. Being out on the road most of the time definitely had its drawbacks.

"Let's grab a beer and head on into the family room," he suggested when they finished. "The Rangers are playing the Yankees this afternoon."

"Great!" Nate said enthusiastically. "With that sixty-inch television screen and the surround sound, it's going to feel like we're in the stadium."

"Why don't we make that a can of soda or a glass of iced tea." Jaron shook his head. "And don't hold out for a beer, Sam, because it ain't happening, bro. I'm not doing anything to make Bria mad at me."

Sam couldn't help laughing as they walked into the family room. "Don't tell me you're afraid of my wife. She's barely five and a half feet tall and all of a hundred and ten pounds soaking wet."

"We're not exactly afraid of Bria," Ryder explained, grinning. He sat back in one of the chairs and stretched out his long legs to prop them on the ottoman. "But we're not stupid, either. We know better than to get on her bad side. She's one of the best cooks in the whole damn state and we don't want to run the risk of her not making any more birthday dinners."

"Mariah's pies were good, too," Jaron added, sitting down in one corner of the big leather couch.

Sam and his other four brothers exchanged amused glances as they all found seats. "When are you going to give that girl a chance and take her out?" Lane finally asked, grinning. "You know she'd go in a heartbeat."

"She's just a kid," Jaron scoffed. "I'm way too old for her."

"In case you haven't noticed, Methuselah, she's a grown woman now," Nate pointed out. "And a damn fine-looking one at that."

"You stay away from her, Nate," Jaron warned. "You're too old for her, too."

The hard edge in Jaron's voice had them all raising their eyebrows, but before any of them could react, T.J.'s cell phone rang. From his terse responses, Sam could tell the news wasn't good.

"That was my ranch foreman," T.J. said, cursing vehemently as he clipped his cell phone back on to his belt. "The neighbor's stallion jumped the fence again and spoiled two more of my mares."

Raising champion reining horses, T.J. had been complaining for the past year about the woman's stallion coming over to romance his mares. "If that woman doesn't keep her stud on her side of the fence and away from my herd of mares—"

"I think the man is protesting a little too much," Lane interrupted, wearing a knowing grin.

"Give it up, T.J.," Nate teased. "You like when that stud jumps the fence just so you have an excuse to see his owner."

T.J. looked fit to be tied. "A jackass will sprout wings and start flying before I look forward to being in the same county with that woman. She just flat rubs me the wrong way."

As they continued to laugh and catch up with each other, Sam's thoughts kept straying to the woman down at the creek. It was clear that Bria liked doing things for others and that it made her feel good. He had no idea why he hadn't understood that about her before today, but for the first time in their marriage, he began to see what she meant about wanting him to let her do things for him. It gave her a sense of purpose and she thrived on that. But he had been so determined not to be anything like his lazy, irresponsible father, he had taken that away from her. He had viewed her concern and doing little things like bringing him breakfast in bed as her thinking of him as weak and pathetic.

Maybe that was the direction he should take in starting to make things right between them. Maybe if he relied on her a little more, let her do more for him and allowed her to see that he appreciated the care she so selflessly wanted to give, she might have a change of heart.

He took a deep breath. It wasn't going to be an easy thing for him to do after a lifetime of being fiercely independent, but at this point, it sure as hell couldn't hurt to try.

By the time Sam's brothers and Mariah waved goodbye and drove from the ranch yard later that evening, Bria had mixed emotions about the day. She had loved having family around, loved watching the closeness Sam and his brothers shared. But it saddened her to think this was probably the last time she and Mariah would be included in one of their birthday celebrations.

"Thanks, sweetheart," Sam said, putting his arm around her shoulders as they stood on the porch watching the taillights fade into the evening darkness.

"No need to thank me," she said, meaning it. "You know I enjoy getting together with family."

"What do you say to turning off the lights and heading up to bed?" He kissed the top of her head. "You're bound to be bone tired and I know I am."

She was extremely tired, but her exhaustion had nothing whatsoever to do with cooking a big meal and everything to do with the man holding her so snuggly to his side. For the past several nights she had lain awake in his arms, thinking about what could have been and fighting the overwhelming desire to turn to him, to have him love her once again as only he could. But that wouldn't make their problems go away and would only make it more difficult for her to leave once Sam recovered his memory.

"I was thinking that I might read for a while to wind down," she said, hoping he would go upstairs without her. If she waited until he went to sleep, maybe she could go to bed in the guest bedroom and actually get some much-needed sleep. "But you should go on and get your rest."

Sam didn't look pleased, but giving her a quick kiss, he started toward the door. He hadn't gone more than a couple of steps when he stopped suddenly and started to sway.

"You're light-headed again, aren't you?" she said, rushing to his side.

When he closed his eyes and put his arm around her shoulders to lean against her, he took a deep breath. "I'll be okay in a second or two." A muscle along his jaw worked furiously as he fought the vertigo. "I guess

I might have done a little too much the past couple of days," he finally said, opening his eyes.

"Can you make it into the house?" she asked.

Her concern increased when he gave her a short nod, then closed his eyes against another wave of dizziness. What if he became dizzy and fell down the stairs as they tried to get to the bedroom for him to lie down?

"Maybe you should sleep downstairs tonight, Sam."

He shook his head. "I'll make it, sweetheart."

Her heart felt as if it was in her throat until they reached the top of the stairs and entered the master suite. As soon as he was sitting on the side of the bed, she released the snaps on his chambray shirt and slid it from his broad shoulders.

"I can undress myself," he said tightly.

"I'm not going to argue with you, Sam." She pulled off his boots and socks, then tossed them aside. Reaching for his belt, she made quick work of unbuckling the tooled-leather strap. "Do you think you can stand up for me to get you out of your jeans?"

"There's not a man alive who would say no to that, sweetheart," he said, slowly rising to his feet and placing his hands on her shoulders to steady himself.

She shook her head. "Really, Sam? You're thinking about making love even now when you're so light-headed you can barely stand up? Is that all men think about?"

"It's a guy thing, sweetheart."

"It must be," she muttered as she unbuttoned his waistband, carefully lowered the zipper at his fly, then pushed the denim down his muscular thighs. Even though he was trying to make light of the situation, the fact that he was willingly allowing her to undress him caused her concern to increase. It was something he normally wouldn't even consider unless they were getting ready to make love.

"Do you want me to call Nate or one of the others?" she asked, wishing his brothers hadn't already left.

"No, the dizziness is letting up," he said, stepping out of his jeans. "I just need to stretch out for a while."

This bout of vertigo had been worse than any of the others and she needed to check the instructions they were given when he was discharged from the hospital. She might need to call the doctor or take Sam to the hospital E.R. "Do you think you'll be all right while I go downstairs for a minute to get the discharge papers?"

Sam caught her hand in his. "Sweetheart, don't worry. It was just a little dizzy spell. I'm okay now."

Bria searched his face. His eyes were clear and focused and he didn't seem to be in any pain. "Are you sure?"

He nodded. "As long as I have you with me, I'll be just fine."

Sam's words caused her chest to tighten and tears to burn at the backs of her eyes. Why couldn't he have said something like that to her during the past three years? Why did he have to wait until their divorce was almost final to come to that conclusion?

Needing a moment to compose herself, she motioned toward the bathroom. "I'm going to go change and brush my teeth. I'll only be a moment."

Bria hurried across the room and barely managed to

get the bathroom door closed before her emotions took over. As tears trickled down her cheeks, she couldn't help thinking about all the times she had longed to hear Sam say those words.

She swiped at her tears with her fingertips and took a deep breath. He might feel that way now, but as soon as he recovered his memory and the doctor released him to go back to work it would all go back to the way it had always been. Sam would go back to traveling non-stop with his rodeo-livestock company and she would be left alone to wait until he graced her with his presence once again. It was something she couldn't allow herself to forget. Her survival depended on it.

With her perspective restored, Bria washed her face and changed into her nightshirt. She was facing another sleepless night in Sam's arms—wanting to turn to him, knowing she couldn't let herself do that.

Taking a deep breath, she opened the door and walked into the bedroom to lie down on her side of the bed. "Any more dizziness?"

"No." He reached to pull her over to him. "I'm just tired and need to hold my wife for a while. Do you have any idea how hard it was not to be able to touch you like this today?" he asked, sliding his hand up beneath the tail of her nightshirt.

Sam's callused palm skimming along her thigh, then up over her stomach and ribs to cup her breast sent a jolt of need streaking from the top of her head all the way to her toes. With the exception of the other morning when he had pulled her into bed with him, it had been months since he had touched her like this and heaven help her, it felt absolutely wonderful.

"S-Sam…I can't—"

"Still not a good time?" he asked, nibbling tiny kisses from the side of her neck down to the rapidly beating pulse at the base of her throat.

"I…uh, no." She was extremely glad he had supplied her excuse for her because at the moment she couldn't remember a single reason why they shouldn't make love.

She could feel his lips smiling against the overly sensitive skin along her collarbone. "Like I told you the other morning, Bria, I don't have to be inside you to make love to you."

Her pulse sped up at the promise she heard in his slightly hoarse voice. But when Sam teased the tight tip of her breast with his thumb as he kissed his way along her jaw to her lips, her heart felt as if it might leap from her chest. There wasn't a doubt in her mind that he meant every word he had said. He was going to drive her to the brink and she wasn't sure she would have the willpower to call a halt to it.

Somehow, she had to find the strength to stop him before she lost what little sense she had left. "I love the way you make…me feel, Sam," she said honestly. "But I'm really…exhausted."

She wasn't lying. He had always made her feel that she was the only woman he wanted, the only woman he cherished. And she *was* tired. Just not as tired as she was letting on.

Turning her to her side so they were face-to-face, he lightly kissed her lips. "I understand." He pressed his lower body into the cradle of her hips. "I just don't want you to forget how hot you make me and how much I want you."

The feel of his strong arousal caused an answering tightness in the pit of her stomach and she couldn't have stopped her tiny moan of need if her life depended on it.

"Shh, sweetheart." Cupping her cheek, he tilted her head back until their gazes met. "It will only be another day or two and I'll be able to love every inch of you. And when I'm finished, there won't be a doubt in your mind what you do to me and how much I need you." He gave her a kiss that curled her toes. "Now, let's get some rest. We've both had a big day."

Bria watched Sam close his eyes and in no time his even breathing indicated that he had drifted off to sleep. She knew she wasn't going to be that lucky.

Wrapped securely in his arms, with her head pillowed on his bare shoulder, it took everything she had in her not to give in to the overwhelming temptation of waking him and asking him to make love to her. He wanted her and she wanted him and nothing would please her more than for Sam to make her forget the reasons why she felt she had no alternative but to divorce him.

Squeezing her eyes shut, she tried to will away the impulse to give their relationship one more try. It would be easy to tear up the divorce papers and when he regained his memory tell him that she wanted to see if they could work things out. Did she have the courage to risk getting her heart broken again if they couldn't?

In the past, no matter how many times she had tried

to explain how she felt to him and what she needed from their marriage—from him—Sam had insisted that everything he did was for her and their future family and hadn't been willing to compromise. He had promised to stop traveling one day, but that day never seemed to come. Could she survive having to go through a painful breakup a second time if things didn't work out for them?

As she lay there staring at the man she had loved from the moment they met, Bria bit her lower lip to keep it from trembling. She wasn't sure about anything anymore. But one thing that was certain and remained a complete mystery to her was the fact that no matter how disillusioned she had become with the state of their marriage, she still wanted him with a fierceness that stole her breath.

Six

Sitting at the desk in his office, Sam stared off into space as he tried to think of ways to turn things around with Bria before he had to tell her that the majority of his memory had returned. There were still some areas that remained a little foggy, but for the most part the dizzy spell he had experienced the night before had restored the events of the past six months—enough so for him to realize that if he didn't do something, and damn quick, he was going to lose her.

There were some things she thought were problems in their marriage that he didn't think were problems at all. But the only way to get her to see his side of things would be for them to work together to find a happy medium. He had already conceded that letting her do a few things for him, letting her fuss over him a little, wouldn't be as degrading to his pride as he had once thought. And although he would love to spend more time with her, he needed to get her to see that he had to work, that making a good living for her was his purpose in life. He had tried to tell her before, but this time he had to make her see where he was coming from, had to get her to understand his side of the issue.

But working things out with her wasn't going to happen if she divorced him and moved two hours away to live in Dallas. And it seemed that's what she was hell-bent on doing.

Unfortunately, time wasn't on his side. If he didn't find some way to prove to her that she belonged with him within the next week or two, Bria would leave again, the divorce would be final and this time there wouldn't be a second chance. This time it would be for good.

"Sam, it's such a nice day, would you like to walk down to the creek with me?" Bria asked from the doorway.

When he looked up, his heart stalled. He didn't even want to contemplate what his life would be like without her in it. That's why he had to win her back as soon as possible. The way he saw it, now was as good a time as any to get started.

"Sure," he said, smiling. He wasn't surprised she was going back down to the creek. Sitting under that old cottonwood tree while she read a book had always been one of her favorite things to do on a lazy summer afternoon. "Are you wanting fish for supper?"

"Have you decided to disturb the catfish and his lady friend?" she asked, laughing.

"Maybe we'd better plan on having something else tonight," he said as he turned off his computer and rose to his feet. "I'd hate to ruin their day."

When they walked out of the house and headed down the path behind the barn to Sugar Creek, Sam reached over and took Bria's hand in his. He loved touching her, and the thought of having that privilege taken away from him was more than he wanted to deal with. He had watched her walk out once and it had damn near killed him. He couldn't let it happen again. But what could he do to convince her to stay with him?

He couldn't talk to her about why she felt divorce was the only answer. That would entail letting her know that his memory had returned and once she found out about that, she would pack up and make things final. Besides, just like the first time she left, Bria would want answers about why he hadn't rushed to her side when she had the miscarriage, and those were answers he wasn't yet ready to give her—might never be able to give her.

No, he was going to have to show her that she belonged with him, that she was as vital to him as the air he breathed. He could tell she still cared for him or she wouldn't be with him while he recovered from the accident, nor would she respond to him the way she did when he held her, kissed her. That was in his favor and a pretty good sign that he wasn't going to be fighting a lost cause. Maybe spending time with her the way he was doing now was a start and if he thought about it a little more, he was certain he could think of other ways to convince her not to give up on them.

"Do you have any idea how pretty you look today

in that white sundress?" he asked, bringing her hand
up to his lips to kiss the back of it. Made of some kind
of gauzy fabric, the light summer breeze made the full
skirt flutter around her ankles and it looked almost as
if she floated just above the ground. "You look like an
angel—my angel."

Clearly taken aback, she smiled and shook her head.
"Thank you, but I really hadn't given a lot of thought
to the way I look."

As she handed him the blanket to spread beneath
the cottonwood tree, it bothered him that Bria was surprised he admired the way she looked. It bothered him
more that he couldn't remember the last time he had
actually told her how beautiful he thought she was. He
had always thought she was the prettiest woman he had
ever seen and he had told her he thought she looked
hot, but that wasn't the same as paying her a genuine
compliment.

"If you aren't going to be fishing, what are you going
to do while I read?" she asked, kicking off her sandals,
then lowering herself to sit on the blanket.

He stretched out beside her, then propped his elbow
to rest his chin in his palm as he gazed up at her. "I
don't know." He reached over to draw an invisible heart
on her palm with his index finger. When he heard her
sharp intake of breath, he smiled. "Maybe I'll take a
nap or just lie here and watch you."

"Who are you?" she asked, frowning. "The Sam Rafferty I know would rather do anything than to willingly
be idle for more than five minutes."

Taking her hand in his, he pulled her down to lie beside him. "I've got something to do," he said, wrapping his arms around her. He eased her to her back, then, removing his hat, he leaned over her to brush her mouth with his. "I'm going to kiss my wife and let her know how much she makes me want her."

Before Bria could protest, Sam settled his mouth over hers and savored the sweetness of the most desirable woman he had ever known. At first she lay perfectly still in his arms, but as he traced her soft lips with his tongue, then parted them to slip inside, she put her arms around his shoulders and melted against him.

Thoroughly exploring her soft inner recesses, he stroked her tongue with his and encouraged her to return the favor. When she accepted his invitation and did a little exploring of her own, Sam felt the familiar heat like a flash fire in his loins. No other woman had ever aroused him as fast or to the heights that Bria did. He was harder than hell and aching to join his body with hers.

Sliding his hand beneath the hem of her skirt, he caressed her knee, then skimmed his hand up her smooth thigh. He loved touching her, loved the feel of her satiny skin beneath his palms. She was his woman and all that was good in his life. That he might lose her was something he wouldn't allow himself to consider.

When she shivered, then tangled her legs with his and pressed herself closer, Sam knew she was as turned on as he was. But as ready as he was to make love to her, she wasn't yet ready to take that step with him. Knowing her the way he did, he knew as sure as the sun rose in the east tomorrow morning, Bria would think of her acquiescence as a moment of weakness and regret her actions, instead of viewing it as the natural act between two people who cared deeply for each other. Having her regret anything they shared together was completely unacceptable.

"I don't tell you nearly often enough how honored I am that you're my wife, Bria," he said, easing away from the kiss. He nibbled tiny kisses along her soft cheek to her ear. "Or that I consider myself the luckiest man alive to have you," he whispered.

Raising his head, he watched a small tear slip from the corner of her closed eyes to slowly slide down her temple. As he kissed it away, he hated that his words caused her to cry, hated himself for not telling her sooner and more often. If he had, maybe she wouldn't feel as uncertain as she did now.

"You know, I've been thinking this forced downtime isn't all that bad," he said, smiling at her.

She slowly opened her eyes to stare up at him. "Are you feeling all right?"

Grinning, he nodded. "I like spending time with my best girl."

She looked worried. "Seriously, Sam, are you dizzy or having a headache?"

He couldn't blame her for doubting that he was enjoying his time off. He was a little shocked by it himself.

"I'm fine," he said, kissing her chin. "Do you want to know what I think we need?"

"There's no telling what's running through that mind of yours," she said, sitting up.

"I think we need a date night."

"Are you serious?" Clearly stunned, she shook her head as if trying to clear it. "Where did that come from?"

"You've been wanting us to spend more time together as a couple," he said, remembering one of her main complaints about their marriage. "What better way to do it than to have a date like before we got married? Remember how much fun we had?"

"I remember," she said slowly. "But I wasn't aware that you did."

"I guess all this time here at home with you reminded me," he said, shrugging one shoulder. "Will you go out with me this evening, Mrs. Rafferty?"

She smiled and he could tell she was warming to the idea. "That depends on where you want to go and what you want to do."

"I noticed there's an old classic on one of the satellite movie channels that you mentioned wanting to see and I thought we could make some popcorn and watch it," he said as a plan began to take shape. "Of course, we may have seen it in the past six months and I just don't remember."

"What movie is that?" Her tone didn't sound quite as doubtful.

"It has Clark Gable in it and he's stuck in a motel with some woman." He shook his head as he lay back on the blanket. "I don't remember the title."

"It Happened One Night," she said, smiling. "It's hilarious and I'd love to see it again."

"Sounds like we have a plan, sweetheart," he said, smiling at her.

"A date night with the television in the family room?" she murmured.

He nodded. "Remember the dates we used to have just hanging out at your apartment, watching that old twenty-inch television you used to have?" When she nodded, he folded his arms behind his head and stared up at the tree limbs. "You go ahead and read. I think I'm going to take a nap and rest up for tonight."

"Why would you need to rest up when we're just watching a movie in the family room?" There was a hint of a panic in her voice and he knew she remembered how the evenings had ended when they stayed in at her apartment. He usually spent the night making love to her.

"The movie doesn't come on until after the nightly news," he said reasonably. "I don't want to fall asleep in the middle of it."

Before she could respond, he reached for his hat to cover his eyes and while Bria read, Sam lay on the blanket beside her planning his next move. Seduction was out of the question. For one thing, she was still under the assumption that they were getting a divorce and had gone out of her way to avoid making love with him.

No, his best course of action would be to court her the way he had done when they first met—the way he probably should have done before she left the first time. They had watched movies, gone dancing and spent hours talking about how they wanted their lives to turn out.

All those things had worked for him to get her to say yes when he asked her to be his wife. Maybe they would work again in his effort to get her to stay married to him.

* * *

When the microwave beeped, Bria removed the bag of popcorn and, opening it, poured the fluffy kernels into a bowl. She had no idea what made Sam think back to when they had first started seeing each other, but why did he have to recall that at this stage of the game? Why couldn't he have seen that the many times she had pointed out that she wanted them to spend time together as a couple the way they had in the beginning of their relationship?

"Sweetheart, the movie is about to start," he said from the family room.

"Go ahead and make yourself comfortable on the couch," she called back as she removed a tray from the cabinet to place the bowl of popcorn and two soft drinks on it. "I'll be right there."

When she carried the tray into the family room to set in on the coffee table, Sam was already positioned in a corner of the couch with one long leg stretched out across the cushions. She knew what he intended. He wanted her to sit between his legs and lean back against his chest the way they used to sit and watch movies when they first started seeing each other.

"Hey, where do you think you're going?" he asked when she moved to sit in the chair flanking the couch. He caught her hand as she walked past him. "We can't have a date night if I'm over here and you're over there."

"But I thought you'd be more comfortable—"

"Sweetheart, you've been entirely too worried about my comfort lately." He gave her a grin that caused her lower stomach to flutter with anticipation. "I'll let you know if something goes to sleep and starts hurting."

She wasn't as concerned with something going to sleep as she was with something waking up. But there really wasn't anything she could think of to explain why it was a bad idea to cuddle on the couch with him while they watched the movie.

Sighing, she sat down between his legs and tentatively leaned back against his chest. Sam immediately wrapped his arms around her and held her snuggly to him.

"You're way too tense," he said, kissing the side of her neck. "Relax and lay your head against my shoulder, sweetheart."

When she did as he requested, Bria closed her eyes as his warmth surrounded her. She tried to fight the feeling flowing through her, but there was no denying that in Sam's arms, she felt as if she was where she belonged—where she would always belong.

She told herself she should move, that she should escape the temptation Sam posed to her peace of mind. But for the life of her, she couldn't seem to find the strength. Just as had happened since returning to the ranch, each time he held her, each time he kissed her, the will to resist became that much weaker. This was the man she used to know, the man she fell in love with. She had missed the teasing touches, the subtle hints of how she made him want her and the feel of his body as he let her know his desire was only for her. There hadn't been enough of that in the past couple of years. If there had been, maybe they could have worked past his not being with her when she miscarried and she wouldn't have left him.

Reaching for the bowl to keep from turning to reach for Sam, Bria started to get some popcorn. When her fingers came into contact with Sam's, her heart skipped a beat and she felt as if an electric charge coursed all the way from her fingertips up her arm to her shoulder.

"I think this is yours," he whispered as he brought a piece of popcorn up to her mouth.

A shiver of excitement coursed through her from his warm breath feathering over her ear, and when she opened her mouth, his fingers brushing her lips as he fed her the popcorn caused a tingling sensation to pool in the most feminine part of her. She tried her best to concentrate on the movie and forget about the man holding her so close.

But when he shifted her to cradle her in his arms, then lowered his head to cover her mouth with his, Bria quickly realized she was fighting a losing battle. Heat swirled throughout her body as Sam traced her lips with his tongue, then coaxed her to open for him. As he stroked her with his tongue, the longing in her built to an almost unbearable ache and she couldn't have stopped herself from kissing him back if her life depended on it.

She wanted Sam—had never stopped wanting him. He was the first and only man she had ever been with and the only man she would ever want. But if nothing changed—if everything stayed the same as it had been for the past couple of years between them—could she live the rest of her life that way?

The last thing she had wanted was to end their marriage, but she had been so lonely and unhappy that she felt there was no other alternative. He either didn't understand or was too stubborn to see her point of view when she tried to explain it all to him, and although her heart was telling her to give him another chance, she was afraid they would fall back into the same pattern of her taking a backseat to the Sugar Creek Rodeo Company.

When he eased away from the kiss and raised his head, the heat in his eyes stole her breath. "Sam, I can't—"

"Shh, sweetheart," he interrupted, smiling. "You're missing the movie and this is one of the best parts."

As he helped her sit up and nestled her back against his chest, the feel of his strong arousal pressed to her backside caused a tremor to track its way through her. How was she supposed to concentrate on anything when all she could think about was the man holding her so close? Or the fact that as insane as it was, she wanted him just as much?

"I'm really tired," she said, pretending to yawn. "I think I'll go upstairs to bed, but you go ahead and finish watching the movie."

"No, I'll go upstairs with you," he said, using the remote to turn off the television. He gave her a look that made her feel warm all over. "I'm pretty tired myself."

When he followed her upstairs and they entered the master suite, Bria took a deep breath as she changed into her nightshirt. It was becoming more difficult by the day to think of plausible reasons why they shouldn't make love. Sam wouldn't hear of her sleeping in the bedroom down the hall because she was afraid she might disturb him. And how much longer would she be able to deny the desire building inside herself and keep from turning to him to make love to her?

She tried to remind herself that it was only because the doctor had ordered him not to work that she was getting quality time with him now. But she had missed the easy connection they had when they were dating and in the first months of their marriage. To experience that again was proving to be much more difficult to resist with each passing day.

As they got ready for bed her anxiety increased, and by the time they were lying on the mattress and he took her into his arms, Bria's nerves felt as if they were about to snap.

"Sweetheart, you're way too tense," he said, turning her on her side to face away from him.

The feel of his strong hands gently massaging her shoulder and neck muscles was heaven and hell rolled into one. Any time Sam touched her, her longing for him increased. But as he worked the knots from her muscles, it felt as if he massaged away her will to resist him.

"Sam, I—"

"It's all right," he said, kissing the back of her neck. "I know you're exhausted." He turned her back to face him. "We can make love when you feel more rested."

As he pulled her to him and wrapped his arms around her, Bria wasn't sure whether her sigh was from relief or disappointment. She had started to tell him that she was extremely tired, but she wasn't entirely certain she wouldn't have asked him to make love to her. It had been so long since she had shared that intimacy with Sam and no matter that none of the issues between them had been resolved, she missed sharing that with him.

Relaxed from his soothing touch and secure in his arms, Bria felt the peacefulness of sleep begin to overtake her. There would be plenty of time tomorrow to think about the disparity between what her heart wanted and what her mind was telling her to do. At the moment, she felt she was where she belonged and that was all that mattered.

The next afternoon as he walked back to the house, Sam smiled as he thought about his date night with Bria. He could tell she was waging a battle within herself, and the part of her that still wanted him seemed to be winning. That was all the encouragement he needed to proceed with his plan.

He was going to pull out all the stops to get her to stay at Sugar Creek Ranch. After giving it serious thought, he had come up with a project that he was certain would make her happy. That's why he had snuck out to spend the entire morning down by the creek and couldn't wait to show her the surprise he had for her.

"Bria, sweetheart, could you come here a minute?" he called as he entered the back door.

"Sam? Are you all right?"

He heard her hurrying down the hall toward the kitchen and knew she had to have been worried about him. He had told her he was going to the barn to talk to the ranch foreman about some new bucking horses and she had probably called to check on him.

"I couldn't be better," he assured her.

"Where have you been?" she asked when she rushed up to him. "I called the barn a few minutes ago and Roy Lee said he hadn't seen you."

Sam could see the worry in her eyes and automatically put his arms around her to hold her close. He knew he shouldn't be elated by her obvious concern for him, but it was further proof that he wasn't fighting a lost cause.

"I'm fine, Bria. I didn't mean to upset you." His spirits soared when she put her arms around his waist and hugged him back. "I've been down by the creek."

She leaned back to give him a disapproving look. "What were you doing down there? You know someone is supposed to be with you when you go that far."

"Bria, I haven't had a dizzy spell in the past few days and I don't need a babysitter. But I don't want to talk about that now." Smiling, he took her hand in his and started for the door. "I have something I want to show you."

"At the creek?" she asked as she followed him. "What is it?"

"If I told you, it wouldn't be a surprise," he said, grinning as they walked down the path toward Sugar Creek.

When they reached the cottonwood tree, she frowned as she looked around. "I don't see anything different."

"Look closer," he said, pointing toward some stakes with heavy cord strung between them. "Isn't that where

you said you thought would be a nice place for a gazebo with a swing?"

Her confused expression turned to surprise, then one
of delight. "Are you really planning to have one built?"

Stepping up behind her, he wrapped his arms around
her waist and pulled her back against his chest. "It's
what you mentioned you thought would be nice, isn't
it?"

"Yes, but that was right after we got married that
I talked about it." She shook her head. "I thought you
had forgotten."

"Oh, I didn't exactly forget," he said, nibbling kisses
along the delicate shell of her ear. "I just never seemed
to have the time while I was home to call a contractor
and get the work started."

He knew the moment the words left his mouth that
he must have touched a nerve by the way her body stiffened. "It wasn't that you didn't *have* the time, Sam. It
was more like you wouldn't *take* the time." She pulled
from his arms. "There's a big difference."

"I'm taking the time now," he pointed out, wondering how things could have gone downhill so damn fast.
She had seemed genuinely happy about him building
the gazebo for her and now she looked as if she was
angry with him. "Don't you still want it?"

"I didn't say I wanted it to begin with, only that I
thought it would be nice. But that's not the point." She
closed her eyes as if trying to hold on to her patience.
When she opened them, she shook her head. "We both
know that you were forced to take the time off. It's not
like you did it voluntarily. And the only reason you're

thinking about building it now is because you're bored and want something to do. As soon as you're cleared to go back out on the road with your livestock company, you'll forget all about it."

Stuffing his hands into the front pockets of his jeans, Sam shrugged. "It doesn't matter whether this little vacation was forced on me or not, I'm taking the time to do it now." He stepped forward to put his index finger beneath her chin and tilt her head up until their eyes met. "It's something you'd like and it *will* get done, Bria. I've made sure you have everything you want and I'm not about to stop doing that now."

She stared at him for several long moments before she turned and started walking back toward the house. "Whatever you say, Sam."

As he fell into step beside her, he wisely let the matter drop. Bria had her mind made up and nothing he could say would change it. Besides, she would see soon enough that he meant what he said when the construction crew showed up and started building the gazebo.

But it bothered him that she doubted he would see the project through to the end. He had bent over backward to see that he got her everything she had ever mentioned she thought would be nice or he thought she might like to have. She had mentioned she didn't have time to read as much as she would like, so he had hired Rosa to do the cooking and cleaning. When she said the road leading to the house was a little bumpy, he had a crew come in and put down an asphalt driveway the half mile from the main road up to the house. She saw a necklace and earrings in a magazine she thought was pretty and two days later she was wearing them. What more did she want from him?

He supposed he could point out all the things he had done for her, all the ways he had shown her how much she meant to him. But that just wasn't his style. Hell, she knew all that and it hadn't made a difference three months ago. Why would it make a difference now?

On their way to the house, he motioned toward the barn. "I think I'll check in with Roy Lee about the new string of bucking horses. They should be ready by the time the doctor releases me for work."

"You do that, Sam," she said, staring straight ahead.

Watching her walk the rest of the way to the house, he shook his head. Bria was still in a snit and he didn't have a clue why. Maybe if he gave her a little space, she would calm down and see that everything he did was for her. And in the meantime, he hoped to think of something that would restore her good mood and put his plan to show her that they belonged together back on track.

Seven

As Bria stood at the stove, stirring a pot of beef stock, she couldn't help wondering why Sam had thought about building the gazebo now. It had been the better part of three years since she mentioned that spot down by the creek would be a nice place to have one.

Sighing, she walked into the pantry to get several potatoes, then, placing them in the sink, took some carrots from the crisper in the bottom of the refrigerator to rinse them. She wasn't at all proud of herself for becoming angry with Sam when he took her down to the creek to show her where he was planning to build the gazebo. He had only been trying to do what he thought would make her happy. And she truly did appreciate the gesture. But she had never asked for anything of him but his time. Why couldn't he see that just being with him was more important to her than anything else?

When she heard him walk across the back porch, she took a deep breath and turned to face the door. She owed him an apology. For the past couple of days, he had been the husband she always dreamed of and it wasn't his fault that she still harbored resentment from trying to explain what she needed from him over the past couple of years. He hadn't gotten her meaning all those times. It was unfair for her to expect him to understand it now.

"Sam, I'm—"

"Bria, I didn't mean to—"

They both stopped for a moment to stare at each other.

"I'm sorry about earlier. I thought the gazebo would make you happy. I didn't mean to upset you," he said, breaking the uneasy silence. He moved the hand she hadn't noticed him holding behind his back and held out a beautiful bouquet of colorful wildflowers. "Since you won't hear of me driving yet, I couldn't go up to Stephenville to a flower shop. But I thought you might like these."

The sincerity in his voice and the hopeful look on his face caused tears to fill her eyes. "Sam, you don't have to apologize," she said, shaking her head as she took the flowers. "It's my problem. I shouldn't have—"

"Let's just forget it," he said, wrapping his arms around her. "I know how difficult it's been on you since the accident and how much stress you've been under."

His understanding caused her to feel even worse and she couldn't stop the tears from spilling down her cheeks. "It was my...fault, Sam. I shouldn't have—"

He pulled her close and held her to his broad chest. "Please don't cry, sweetheart."

She knew he hated seeing her cry, and just knowing that she was making him uncomfortable caused her tears to fall even faster. Sam was a good man and the love of her life. It had taken every ounce of strength she possessed to leave him the first time. How would she ever be able to do it a second time? Did she even want to try?

She knew she couldn't return to the way things had been before she left him, but she wasn't certain she could face a future without him, either. It was something she was going to have to give serious thought to, but it would have to wait until her perspective was restored. She was certain that being in his arms again was clouding her judgment and something as important as the decision of whether or not to stay with him in order to give their relationship another chance needed to be made with a clear head.

"I—I'm sorry," she said, sniffing back the last of her tears. "I didn't mean to start sobbing. I know it makes you uncomfortable."

Releasing her, he put a bit of space between them, then gently framed her face with his hands. "It's all right, Bria." He gave her a smile filled with such understanding it was all she could do not to burst into tears all over again. "I couldn't care less about my comfort. All I want is for you to be happy."

Before she could respond, he stepped back and, taking the flowers from her, walked over to one of the cabinets and opened it. "Where's the green vase you used to keep up here?" he asked.

"I'm not sure," she said evasively. She couldn't tell him that it was in Dallas with the rest of her things. "Just get one of the large iced-tea glasses and put the flowers in that."

"We'll have to get you another vase," he said, filling a glass with water and putting the flowers in it. He sat it in the middle of the table, then turning, nodded toward the stove. "What can I do to help get supper ready?"

Bria barely managed to keep her mouth from dropping open. Sam hadn't offered to help her in the kitchen since they were first married. Then after he hired Rosa to do most of the cooking, Bria didn't often have the opportunity to cook, let alone have him help her. It was just one more thing that she had missed during the past three years.

"I was getting ready to peel a few potatoes and carrots for the stew I'm going to make," she said, walking over to finish rinsing the vegetables she had put into the sink earlier. "Would you like to take care of that while I cut up an onion or two?"

"Hand me a knife," he said, smiling.

"By the way, I called Rosa and gave her another week off with pay," Bria said conversationally. She really hadn't had a choice. As sweet as she was and as much as Bria loved her, the older woman was also a chatterbox and would no doubt end up telling Sam things he needed to remember on his own.

Sam gave her a smile that caused her knees to wobble. "Good idea. I don't have to watch where I touch you or how much I kiss you with no one else around."

"You're hopeless," she said, feeling a little breathless.

"I can't help it if you make me hotter than a two-dollar pistol on a Saturday night," he said, grinning.

As they worked side by side to make the stew, Bria spent the majority of her time waging a battle within herself as she tried to decide what to do. Sam was unaware of how things between them had deteriorated after she had the miscarriage. Until he remembered all that had taken place leading up to her filing for divorce, she really couldn't discuss the problems in their marriage with him to see if they could work things out.

The sound of the knife Sam had been using to peel potatoes dropping to the countertop and his graphic curse drew Bria out of her disturbing introspection. "What's wrong?"

"Oh, it's just a little cut," he said, turning on the faucet to run water over the laceration. The sight of blood dripping steadily from his thumb told her it was more serious than he was letting on.

"Let me see," she said, reaching for a towel to blot away some of the blood.

He hesitated a moment, then to her surprise held out his hand for her to assess the wound. Normally he would take care of a cut on the hand himself by wrapping it with something to stop the bleeding, then go on with whatever he had been doing.

"I think you're going to need a couple of stitches," she said, examining his thumb.

At first he shook his head, then pausing for a moment, he shocked her when he nodded. "It probably wouldn't hurt for you to drive me over to the walk-in clinic in Beaver Dam."

Quickly shutting off the stove and grabbing her purse, Bria drove Sam to the clinic. She still had a hard time believing that he willingly took her advice about going to the doctor. It was something that he never would have done before his accident. Normally, he was the type of man who resisted medical attention of any kind unless he was unconscious or so ill that he couldn't function. She had only seen him that way once before— when he suffered the concussion almost two weeks ago.

Two hours later as they walked out of the clinic with Sam sporting four stitches in the fleshy part of his right thumb, she pointed toward the roadhouse down the street. "It's getting late. Would you like to get something to eat at the Broken Spoke before we start home?"

He shook his head. "I think I'd just like to go home." Grinning, he took her hand in his as they walked across the clinic parking lot toward her SUV. "I'd rather be alone with you than spend the evening in a roomful of hot-to-trot cowboys watching you like they want to make you their next meal."

Bria's pulse sped up at the heated look in his dark blue eyes. "Don't you think that's a bit of an exaggeration?"

"Not at all, sweetheart." He opened the driver's door for her, then helped her into the Explorer. "I've seen the way those guys look at you and I don't feel like sharing the view." He gave her a kiss that curled her toes inside her cross trainers. "Tonight, that's for my eyes only."

When he walked back around the SUV and got into the passenger seat, neither had a lot to say as she drove the twenty miles back to the ranch. All Bria could think about was what would happen once they got home. She had seen that look in Sam's eyes too many times not to know that he wanted her. And heaven help her, she wanted him just as much.

But she wasn't sure she was ready to commit herself to giving them another chance. It would be so easy to give in to the overwhelming temptation of forgetting about the divorce and make love with Sam. But nothing had been resolved between them. Could she live with the heartache and regret if things didn't work out? Was she prepared to go back to being the wife who only saw her husband a few times a month when he stopped by on the way to the next rodeo?

She didn't have any answers and until she did, it would be unfair to both of them for her to throw caution to the wind. That would only set up both of them for the devastation of going through another breakup.

It had nearly destroyed her to leave him the first time. She knew for certain she wouldn't be able to survive a second time.

Sam sat in the family room impatiently waiting for Bria to finish washing the supper dishes. He had spent the entire afternoon trying to think of something that would make her happy and never suspected that cutting his thumb would give him an idea that was sure to please her.

Earlier, when they walked out of the clinic and he

had looked down the street at the Broken Spoke, he knew that taking Bria dancing was the answer. The first time he ever saw her had been at a party for the riders and personnel after a rodeo in Amarillo. She had been line dancing with her sister, Mariah, and some of their friends, and from the moment he laid eyes on her, Sam knew Bria was the one for him.

He supposed they could have danced after having supper at the roadhouse in Beaver Dam, but having a roomful of men ogling his wife wasn't part of his plan for the evening, nor did he want to waste a half hour for the drive back home. That's why he had declined eating at the Broken Spoke in favor of coming home to be alone with Bria. And now that he had her favorite CD queued up on the player, the chairs moved out of the way and a couple of candles lit, he couldn't wait for her to join him in his impromptu dance hall.

When he heard Bria walking toward the family room, Sam picked up the remote for the CD player and turned it on. As the first notes of the romantic country tune began, he stood up and turned to watch her walk into the room.

She was the most beautiful woman he had ever seen and each day they were together he fell just a little bit harder, wanted her just a bit more than he had the day before. He took a deep breath. His plan to win her back had to work. He didn't even want to think about the living hell he would go through if he couldn't.

"What's this?" she asked, looking around at the candles and at the furniture he had moved.

Sam walked over to her, then leading her back to

the area he had cleared, he took her hands in his and raised them to his shoulders. Wrapping his arms around her waist, he drew her close. "I want to dance with my wife."

To his satisfaction, she smiled and began swaying with him in time to the music. "What made you decide we need to dance?" she murmured against his shoulder.

"You like to dance and I like to do things that make you happy," he said, kissing the top of her head.

He heard her catch her breath a second before she leaned back to look up at him. The uncertainty in the depths of her green eyes caused a knot to form in his stomach. Without a second thought he lowered his head and covered her mouth with his. He wanted to wipe away whatever indecision and doubts she had about staying with him, wanted to remind her that they belonged together.

When he deepened the kiss, Bria's soft sigh as she pressed herself closer caused his heart to pound against his rib cage and a spark to ignite in his lower belly. Her response and the fact that it had been months since he'd made love to her sent his temperature soaring. But his need for her could wait. Tonight was all about her, all about making her realize that no matter what problems they had experienced in the past, what they had together was worth saving.

He would have tried to remind her of all that three months ago when she left him, but he had been out on the road for over a week and when he returned, she hadn't given him the chance. She was so upset and so intent on leaving, he knew she wouldn't have heard a word he said, anyway. And anything he did at that point, any gesture he made to show her how much he cared, she would have viewed as manipulation. Then later, when she might have been more receptive to listening to him, it had come down to a matter of pride. He had never groveled for anything in his life, even before he'd come to the Last Chance Ranch, and although it had damn near killed him to watch her walk away, he hadn't been able to bring himself to beg her to stay.

But tonight nothing was going to stop him from showing her exactly how much he needed her, how much he cared.

Ending the kiss, he smiled down at her. "Do you remember the night we met, sweetheart?"

"How could I forget?" she asked breathlessly. "You bribed the band to play nothing but slow songs for the last half of the party."

"That's because I wanted to hold you like I'm doing now." He grinned. "If I remember correctly, you weren't complaining."

Her smile sent a shaft of need straight to the region south of his belt buckle. "No, I don't suppose I was."

"I was the envy of every guy in the room that night, too," he whispered close to her ear. He felt her body tremble and knew she was remembering the magic that had surrounded them that evening. "And whenever we go out anywhere together, I still am."

They fell silent for several moments as the dreamy love song surrounded them and Sam had to fight to keep his body in check. He wanted her more with each passing second and it was becoming increasingly more difficult to hide it. But he was waiting for an indication from her that her desire for him was just as strong.

When the song ended and Bria gazed up at him, his heart stuttered. "Sam, will you please kiss me the way you did that night?"

"Sweetheart, I thought you'd never ask," he said, lowering his mouth to hers.

As soon as their lips met, his body tightened and the need to possess her became more than he could fight. He wanted to make her his once again, needed to show her that together they were part of something much larger than themselves.

Coaxing her to open for him, he tightened his arms around her and slipped his tongue inside to stroke and tease. Her response was everything he hoped for when she clutched at his shirt and sagged against him.

Without a second thought, he tugged her light green tank top from the waistband of her jeans and slid his hand up along her slender ribs to the underside of her breast. Her smooth skin beneath his palm felt like the finest satin and he longed to touch every inch of her. As he moved his hand to cover her breast, he pressed his lower body to hers and allowed her to feel what she did to him and how much she made him want her. To his satisfaction, instead of trying to put distance between them, she moaned softly and tried to move closer.

Easing away from the kiss, Sam gazed down at the passion in her emerald eyes and the blush of desire on her creamy cheeks. She was his woman, his other half, and he needed to show her how vital she was in his life.

"Let's go upstairs, sweetheart."

She stared at him for several long seconds before she finally spoke. "There's something we should talk about first."

"Do you want me, Bria?"

He watched her close her eyes as if she was waging a battle within herself a moment before opening them to slowly nod. "Yes, Sam. I want you. But I really need to tell you—"

"There's nothing that can't wait until tomorrow," he said, placing his index finger to her lips. He knew she wanted to discuss her leaving and their pending divorce, but there would be plenty of time for that later, after he had shown her how good they still were together. "Tonight is all about us and what we have together."

Before she could comment, he blew out the candles he had lit earlier, then putting his arm around her shoulders, he guided her toward the stairs. Neither spoke as they climbed the steps and walked down the upstairs hall toward the master suite. Words were unnecessary. It was time to show her that what they shared was precious and worth whatever it took to save it.

When Sam opened the door to the master suite, Bria knew she was taking a big risk. He couldn't remember and they hadn't discussed the breakup of their marriage or what she needed from him as her husband. But she could no longer ignore what her heart had tried to tell her from the moment she had watched the bull run him down. Sam was her soul mate, the man she had pledged her life to, and if there was any possibility of them working things out, she had to try again.

Maybe the time he had to take off from work had shown him how good their lives could be if he was home more. Maybe now he would understand what she meant when she told him it was the simple things that made her happiest, that just being with him was enough for her.

A shiver of anticipation shot through her when Sam led her over to the bed, then switching on the lamp on the bedside table, turned to face her. The look in his heated blue gaze stole her breath as he bent to remove her cross trainers and his boots and socks.

"I don't want to miss a single moment of loving you," he said, his low drawl causing a tingling sensation to start in the most feminine part of her. He stepped forward and, cupping her face with his hands, kissed her so tenderly Bria felt as if she might melt into a puddle at his feet. "And when I get finished, I'm going to start all over again."

Her heart sped up. The promise in his words and his intense expression left no doubt in her mind that he meant everything he said. Heaven help her, that was exactly what she wanted him to do.

Sliding his hands over her shoulders, then down her arms to catch her hands in his, he smiled. "I think we're a little overdressed for what I have in mind, Mrs. Rafferty."

"What do you think will remedy the problem?" she asked, returning his smile.

"I was thinking that you might be more comfortable without this," he said, catching the hem of her tank top in his hands.

She didn't have to think twice about raising her arms and allowing him to whisk it away. His gaze caught and held hers when he reached to release the front clasp of her bra, then parting the scrap of silk and lace, he slid the straps down her arms and tossed it aside. The first touch of his palms cupping her, the contrast of his work-hardened calluses against her softer skin, sent waves of heat flowing from the top of her head to the tips of her toes. But when he teased her nipples with the pads of his thumbs, Bria closed her eyes and savored his touch and the delicious longing that he was building inside her.

Unable to remain passive a moment longer, she reached for the top snap on his chambray shirt. "This looks like it might feel better off than on."

Opening the metal closure, she trailed her finger through the light sprinkling of hair on his chest to the next snap and the next, treating him to the same sweet torture he had put her through. She felt him shudder and, glancing up, watched him clench his teeth when she reached the snap just above his belt buckle.

"Does that feel good, Sam?"

"If it felt any better, you'd have to bury me," he said, chuckling as he quickly tugged the tail of his shirt from the waistband of his jeans. "But believe me, sweetheart. I'd be going out of this world a happy man."

Smiling, she pushed the garment from his wide shoulders, then down his arms to join her tank top and bra at their feet. She loved his body, loved the wide angles and thick pads of muscle. Tracing the lines of his taut abdomen, she made her way to the line of dark brown hair arrowing down from his navel to disappear into his low-slung jeans.

His sharp intake of breath when she worked the button loose at the top of the denim band was her reward and, encouraged, Bria toyed with the tab at the top of his fly. "Would you like me to continue?" she asked, glancing up at him.

He nodded. "If you don't, I just might lose what little mind I have left."

Slowly, carefully, she lowered the zipper over the bulge straining at his boxer briefs. "You seem to have a little problem, Mr. Rafferty."

The sound of his low chuckle sent a shiver of excitement straight up her spine. "Little? You're lucky I'm not an insecure man, sweetheart."

"Little might have been the wrong word," she agreed, smiling back.

When she touched the hard ridge, Sam's grin quickly faded and a groan rumbled up from deep in his chest. He quickly brushed her hands away and, shoving his jeans and boxer briefs down his muscular thighs, kicked them toward the growing pile of their clothing.

Bria's breath caught at the magnificent sight of her husband. Sam was the embodiment of the perfect man, at least the perfect man for her. With wide shoulders, well-defined muscles and narrow hips, he had the physique of an athlete. Her gaze drifted lower and her heart skipped several beats. Although they had been together for five years and married for three, the sight of his full arousal never failed to send her pulse racing and an empty ache to form deep in her lower belly.

Stepping forward, he didn't say a word as he reached for the waistband of her jeans and quickly released the button and lowered the zipper. Slowly sliding his hands along her hips, he pushed the denim and her panties down her legs until she stepped out of them.

"You're so beautiful," he said, his voice hoarse as he took her into his arms.

The moment his hair-roughened flesh met her softer feminine skin, the entire length of Bria's body felt as if it had touched an electric current. Closing her eyes, she reveled in their differences and the unique contrast of man to woman.

"Sweetheart, I think we'd better lie down while we still have the strength to get into bed," he whispered as he nibbled kisses from below her ear to her shoulder.

Not sure her legs would support her much longer, she reached to pull back the comforter and got into bed. He quickly stretched out beside her and pulled her back into his arms.

"Your body feels so damn good against mine," he said, his voice low and intimate. "I'm not sure I'm going to be able to make this last as long as I'd like, Bria."

She couldn't have agreed more. "Please make love to me, Sam," she begged.

"Not until I'm sure you're ready for me," he answered, sending a wave of goose bumps shimmering across her overly sensitized skin.

He moved one of his hands from her back along her side to the swell of her hip. His gentle caress as he slid his palm down to the apex of her thighs was thrilling and sent heat moving through her veins. But when he captured her lips with his as he excited her with his touch, Bria felt as if she might go mad from the longing Sam created.

Needing to explore his body as he explored hers, when she found him to tease and arouse, the emptiness within her grew to an almost unbearable ache. She wanted him, needed him to join their bodies.

"I'm sorry, sweetheart, but I'm not going to be able to last if you keep that up," he said, sounding as if he had run a marathon.

"P-please, Sam," she said, amazed at the desperation she heard in her own voice. "I need you. Now."

When he eased her to her back, then parted her thighs with his knee, she held her breath as she waited for him to make them one. Capturing her gaze with his, he gave her a smile that left no doubt what he meant. "Show me where you want me."

Without hesitation she guided Sam to her, then closed her eyes and wrapped her arms around him as he pressed forward and sank himself deep inside her. The feeling of being filled by him was exquisite and she wanted it to last forever.

"Sweetheart, open your eyes."

When she did as he commanded, she felt branded by the passion and desire she detected in his dark blue gaze. She belonged with Sam. He had claimed her body and soul and she knew in that moment, she wouldn't have it any other way.

As he continued to hold her gaze with his, he slowly began to rock against her and she readily moved with him as the delicious sensations within her began to build. She loved Sam, had never stopped loving him and although they still had issues to work through, she owed it to both of them to try to resolve things between them.

Lost in the magic they created together, all too soon she found herself poised to find the release they both sought. Sam apparently sensed her readiness and increased the rhythm and depth of his thrusts, sending her over the edge.

Heat streaked throughout her entire being and Bria hung on to Sam to keep from being lost. Her body gently caressing his must have triggered his release, because she felt the slight swelling of him within her a moment before he shuddered and she felt the warmth of him filling her with his essence.

As he collapsed on top of her, she relished the weight of his larger body covering hers and, wrapping her arms around him, held him tightly to her. She experienced a moment of panic at the thought that they hadn't used protection, but only briefly. They had both wanted a baby for some time and although they still had problems they needed to work on in their marriage, she could never regret a child born out of the love they shared.

When Sam regained his strength, he tried to roll to her side, but she held him close. She didn't want to lose the connection, the feeling of being one with him.

"Bria, sweetheart, I'm too heavy for you," he said, rolling them both onto their sides to face each other.

"I just like feeling close to you," she said, kissing him until they both gasped for breath.

His throaty laughter as he pressed his lower body closer and him becoming aroused once again sent a delightful tingling sensation over every one of her nerve endings. "Oh, you'll be feeling close to me again soon." He smiled. "Real soon, sweetheart."

Eight

The following morning after the most incredible night of making love to his beautiful wife, Sam leisurely stretched, then rolled over to put his arm around Bria. But when he realized she wasn't in bed beside him, he opened his eyes to look around. Apprehension filled him until he heard the shower running.

His concern quickly turned to satisfaction and, grinning, he got out of bed. Things were going to work out between them just the way he had hoped. He was sure of it. He knew Bria well enough to be certain she wouldn't have made love with him if she intended to go through with the divorce.

Last night he had shown her in several ways how much he cared for her, how he cherished her. Surely now she understood why he worked so hard, why he did everything in his power to give her whatever she wanted. He loved her and wanted to give her her heart's desire.

Quietly entering the bathroom, he enjoyed watching the silhouette of her luscious body through the frosted glass for a moment before walking over to open the shower door. Stepping into the spacious stall, he took her in his arms.

"Good morning, sweetheart."

Her startled squeak quickly turned to a little moan as their water-slick bodies came together. Turning to face him, she put her arms around his waist and kissed his chest.

"Good morning, Mr. Rafferty." She glanced down at his obvious desire for her. "I see you have another problem."

He couldn't seem to stop grinning. "That seems to happen to me every time I'm around you, Mrs. Rafferty."

"Oh, so it's my fault?" she teased, smiling at him.

Her pretty smile sent his blood pressure up a good ten notches. "So what are you going to do about it?" he asked, nodding.

"What would you suggest?" She trailed her finger from the middle of his chest down to his navel, sending blood pulsing through his veins. But when she traced the line of hair down to his sex, then took him in her hand, he felt as if his head might fly right off his shoulders.

"I think what you're doing is a damn good start," he said through gritted teeth.

"Anything else?" she asked, gently caressing the softness below.

His heart felt as if it might jump right out of his chest as she slowly stroked his heated body. He loved when she touched him, loved that she wasn't shy about letting him know what she wanted.

"I think I've had about all of this I can take," he said, taking her hands in his to place them on his shoulders. Wrapping his arms around her, he lifted her and she automatically locked her legs around his waist.

The feel of her breasts pressed to his chest, her hardened nipples scoring his flesh and the warmth of her femininity against his lower belly sent a wave of heat streaking through him at the speed of light. Tightening his arms to hold her to him, he captured her lips with his and as he deepened the kiss to imitate a more intimate coupling, he was rewarded with her soft moan of pleasure.

If her enthusiastic response was any indication, Bria was as turned on as he was and there wasn't a doubt in his mind that he held the most exciting, desirable woman in the world. She was everything good in his life and just knowing that she would be staying with him created a need so strong it damn near buckled his knees.

He broke the kiss to draw in some much-needed oxygen. "Bria, I need you. Now."

"I need you…too," she said breathlessly.

Shifting her in his arms, Sam leaned back against the tiled wall of the shower to brace them, then entered her in one smooth stroke. The look of sheer delight on her beautiful face and the feel of her taking him in, her body clinging to his as if she tried to absorb him almost drove him over the edge.

"Don't move, sweetheart," he commanded. He clenched his teeth and used every ounce of willpower he possessed to maintain what little control he had left. "I don't think either one of us wants this to be over before we even get started."

"You feel so good, Sam," she said, resting her head against his shoulder. "Please, love me."

"I don't think I have a choice," he admitted, moving his lower body against her.

He tried to go slow as he set a rhythmic pace, tried to make the moment last. But wanting her as he did, it was an all but impossible task. After an entire night of loving her, how could he still be so desperate for her?

As he moved inside her, Sam quickly gave up trying to analyze his need and focused on bringing pleasure to the woman in his arms. He knew her body as well, if not better, than his own, and he could tell she was close to reaching the completion they both raced to find.

When he felt her feminine muscles tighten around him, then gently caress him as the passion overtook her, Sam found his own release from the tension holding them captive. As he held her close, he felt as if he might be consumed by the white-hot waves of pleasure surging through him. For what seemed like an eternity, he continued to hold her. He was as reluctant to end their union as she had been the night before.

"Are we going to stay like this?" she asked, lifting her head from his shoulder to smile at him.

He grinned. "I wouldn't complain."

"I wouldn't either." Laughing, she kissed his chin. "But it might make fixing your breakfast a bit difficult."

"You do have a point," he said, reluctantly loosening his hold to lower her to her feet. "I don't know why, but I'm starved this morning."

"Could it be that you expended too much energy last night and this morning?" she asked playfully.

Laughing, he nodded. "That might have something to do with it."

"While you take your shower, I'll go downstairs and see what I can make that will restore some of your strength," she said, opening the shower door.

After Bria toweled herself dry and left the bathroom to get dressed and go downstairs, Sam quickly showered, then wrapping a towel around his waist, stood in front of the mirror to shave. He couldn't seem to wipe the sappy grin from his face. Bria was going to call off the divorce. He was sure of it. He should be cleared to resume work later this afternoon when he saw the neurologist and if they were lucky, last night or this morning, he might have given her the baby they both wanted.

"Life is turning out pretty damn good," he said to the grinning fool staring back at him from the mirror.

Wanting to spend as much time with Bria as he could before Nate showed up a little later to take him to Waco for the doctor's appointment, Sam quickly got dressed and went downstairs. When he entered the kitchen, Bria had just finished making biscuits and gravy, hash browns and bacon.

"Would you like some scrambled eggs to go with the gravy and potatoes?" she asked, smiling at him as she set the plate and a cup of hot coffee at his place on the table.

"I'll be lucky to eat all this," he said, pulling a chair out to sit down.

She frowned. "I thought you said you were really hungry."

Reaching for her, he pulled her down to sit on his lap. "I am, sweetheart, but not for food." He nipped at her delicate earlobe. "I think I'd rather have you for breakfast."

"You're insatiable," she said, putting her arms around his neck.

"I can't help it." He gave her a quick kiss. "You just have that effect on me."

"What time will Nate be here to take you to see the neurologist?" she asked, snuggling against him.

"Midmorning." Stroking her blue-jeans-clad thigh, he asked, "What do you have planned while Nate and I are gone?"

"I thought I'd drive up to Dallas to, um, do a little shopping and check on some things." She kissed the pulse at the base of his throat. "But I'm sure I'll be home in plenty of time to make supper."

Sam knew she was probably going to Dallas to check on the apartment she had rented right after she left Sugar Creek Ranch. He hoped that while she was up there she would give notice to the complex manager that she would no longer be in need of the place. But she wasn't aware that he had recovered his memory and therefore he couldn't ask if that's what she intended to do.

Nor could he tell her about it right away. If he did, he knew for certain she would be upset and insist that he had manipulated the situation, instead of seeing the sincerity in his actions.

"You know we didn't use protection last night or this morning," he said instead. "As many times as we made love, we might have been successful in making you pregnant again." As soon as the word was out of his mouth, Sam knew he had made a grievous error and tipped his hand by the way she went completely still in his arms.

"Again?" She leaned back to look at him. "You remember that I was pregnant six months ago?"

He stared at her for several seconds before he finally nodded. There was no sense in trying to deny it. With the exception of not telling her that his memory had returned, he had never been anything but honest with her and there was no sense in lying to her now—no matter how much trouble he was about to be in.

"How much do you recall?" she asked, standing up to walk over to the kitchen island.

"Pretty much everything," he admitted.

"So you remember that I lost our baby while you were out on the road somewhere, as well as my leaving the ranch and filing for divorce?" she asked, her tone oddly devoid of emotion.

"Yes."

He watched her take a deep breath, then ask him point-blank, "When did you regain your memory, Sam?"

Standing up, he walked over to where she stood.

When he reached out to cup her cheek, she sidestepped his touch. He dropped his hand to his side.

"I started having flashbacks a day or so before Jaron's birthday dinner." He took a deep breath and decided he might as well admit when the rest of his memory came back. "Then that night after everyone left—when I had the dizzy spell and you had to help me to bed—everything else came back."

"Oh, my God, Sam," she gasped. "That was four days ago. Why didn't you…" He watched her shocked expression turn to suspicion, then disillusionment. "How could you do that to me? How could you manipulate me like that?"

"Bria, sweetheart, I didn't—"

"Don't, Sam," she said, cutting him off. "Don't try to justify what you've done." Tears welled up in her eyes and spilled down her cheeks. "You were spending time with me, bringing me flowers, dancing with me, being the kind of husband you thought I wanted you to be just to get me to stay, weren't you? Then you thought once the doctor released you to work, you would go back on the road with your livestock company and everything would return to the way it was before I left. You would be home a few days out of the month and the rest of the time, I would be here at home alone."

"I have to work, Bria." He rubbed at the tension building in the back of his neck. "I need to make sure I can provide you with everything you could ever want or need."

"No, you don't. For one thing, I could care less about what you can buy me. All I've ever wanted was you."

Her green eyes sparkled with anger and he didn't think he had ever seen her as furious as she was at that very moment. "We both know that you've already amassed enough money that you never have to work another day in your life if you don't want to. But I never asked you to quit work completely. All I wanted was for you to cut back on your time away from the ranch and let your wranglers handle things on the road, while you managed it all from here. Which you and I both know you could do." She shook her head. "But that doesn't make me as angry as your deception."

"Bria, I've never deceived you," he insisted, feeling as if his world was starting to crumble around him. "The only thing I'm guilty of is not telling you that I regained my memory."

"That's splitting hairs and you know it, Sam. Your failure to tell me that you remembered what's happened during the past six months is just the same as lying to me." She walked over to where her purse hung on the hook beside the door. Taking it down, she rummaged inside for a moment, then withdrew the keys to her SUV. "I'm going back to Dallas, Sam. The divorce papers are in the upstairs guest bedroom with some of my things. Please sign them and drop them in the mail at your earliest convenience."

"What about your clothes?" he asked as a feeling of déjà vu swept through him. He was watching her walk away from him again and there was nothing he could do or say to stop her. The only difference between this time and three months ago was that there wouldn't be a second chance.

"If you feel like it, you can ship them to me or throw them away." She shook her head as she opened the door. "It really doesn't matter anymore."

"You're my wife. We need to talk about this."

She stopped. "You've never really talked with me, Sam. Why would you start now?"

"What that's supposed to mean?" he asked, frowning.

"We've been together for five years and married for three," she said, sounding resigned. "And in all that time, you've never told me about your childhood, your parents or why you ended up in the care of Hank Calvert at the Last Chance Ranch." She smiled sadly. "I loved you so much, there wasn't anything you could tell me that I wouldn't have understood. But you obviously didn't trust me or my feelings for you enough to give me that opportunity." She bit her lower lip a moment to keep it from trembling. "You wouldn't even talk to me about the loss of our baby. So why would you talk to me about the breakup of our marriage?"

Before he could think of something—anything—to say to get Bria to stay and work things out between them, she opened the back door and walked out of the house and out of his life. And this time he knew it was forever.

When his brother arrived two hours later, Sam sat at the kitchen table, staring into the cup of coffee Bria had poured for his breakfast. It was as cold as the feeling that had filled his soul when he watched her leave a second time.

How could everything have taken such a bad turn in such a short amount of time? he wondered. And how could a man hurt so much inside without dying?

"I didn't see Bria's truck parked outside," Nate said as he walked into the house. "Has she already left for her day of shopping or whatever it is women do when they head for town?"

Sam grunted. "Your guess is as good as mine. I don't know what she's doing right now."

"I can see you're in a good mood," Nate said sarcastically. "What's got your shorts in a wad this morning?"

Sam narrowed his eyes on his younger brother. "How much trouble was it to get Bria to stay with me until my memory returned?"

To Nate's credit he didn't act as if he didn't understand what Sam was talking about. Instead, he pulled out a chair and sat down across the table from him.

"It really wasn't all that hard." His brother shook his head. "She wanted to do whatever she could to help you recover from the accident."

"We would have both been better off if she hadn't bothered and just gone on back to her new life in Dallas." He gave his brother a pointed look. "It would have been easier on all concerned."

"How the hell do you figure that?" Nate asked, frowning. "You couldn't remember that the two of you were having trouble and you wouldn't have believed me or any of the guys if we had told you."

"I would have survived," Sam said, shaking his head. "It wasn't fair to ask that of her. She had to put her new life up in Dallas on hold while she waited on me to re-member we'd called it quits."

"But the divorce wasn't your idea," Nate pointed out. "And I don't think it was what Bria really wanted either. You didn't see how upset she was that first night at the hospital when we didn't know how badly you were injured."

"It doesn't matter. She wants the divorce now," Sam said, rising to scrape his untouched breakfast into the garbage disposal and pour the cold coffee down the drain.

"She's left?" Nate asked.

"Yup."

"So go after her and talk things out," Nate said, his tone emphatic.

"That's the problem," Sam said, shaking his head. "She wants me to tell her things about myself that are better left buried in the past."

"She doesn't know about us?" his younger brother asked, clearly astounded.

"Nope."

"Not even about Mom dying and the authorities having the good sense to take us out of that miserable situation once Dad took off?"

"Nope."

"Hell, Sam, that was eighteen years ago," Nate said, shaking his head. "I figured you had told her all about us and the fact that you attempted to take the rap for me when I tried to hold up that convenience store."

"What good would come of it?" he asked pointedly.

"What harm would it do?" Nate retorted. "We were

both kids and I'm positive Bria would understand. Besides, she's your wife, bonehead. The last I heard, married folks share stuff like that with each other. Why the hell didn't you tell her?"

Sam stared at his younger brother for several long seconds. "What do you know about marriage?"

"Apparently a hell of a lot more than you do." Nate checked his watch. "I think it's about time for us to hit the road, bro," he said, rising to his feet and heading for the back door. "You have a doctor to see and I have a date for lunch and a little TLC from a cute little nurse." He paused to see if Sam followed him. "And while we're driving down to Waco, I think you had better give serious thought to making a trip up to Dallas to tell your wife what you should have told her years ago."

As Sam grabbed his hat from one of the hooks beside the door and walked out to get into Nate's truck, he couldn't stop thinking about what his brother had said. Was Nate right? Would Bria understand that because of their run-in with the law, the Rafferty boys had become charges of Hank Calvert and learned to rise above their raising?

She had just said there wasn't anything he could tell her that would make her stop loving him. Had she really meant it? Did he have the guts to tell her all his dirty little secrets and find out?

Sam stood poised to open the gate as he waited for the rider to climb on the dusty back of Black Mamba, wrap the bull rope around his hand and give the go-ahead nod to turn the bull out into the arena. As dark as the snake he was named for, the bull had never been ridden and with any luck this rider wouldn't be the first. The fewer men who could stay on the animal for the full eight seconds, the bigger demand there would be for his appearance at the national finals at the end of the year.

"Still feeling up to par?" Ryder asked as he positioned himself beside Sam at the chute gate. It had been two weeks since Sam had returned to the rodeo circuit and all his brothers were still asking him if he was doing all right.

"Ask me that one more time and you'll think having a bull chase you around this arena is a picnic compared to dealing with me," Sam warned.

Ryder threw back his head and laughed. "Yup, you're feeling just fine. Nate was right. You're as ornery as a bear with a sore paw." Ryder grinned. "You know, you really should do something about that, bro."

Sam didn't like that his brothers had been discussing his mood, and no doubt the reason for it, behind his back. They all knew Bria had left him again. But instead of leaving him be as they had the first time, they seemed to feel the need to needle him about it with little or no provocation. Of course, none of them were stupid enough to make a direct comment, but the veiled references were there just the same. They all thought he should go to Dallas and try one last time to get her back.

"You just tend to your business and I'll take care of mine," Sam advised, glancing at his watch.

None of them knew, and he wasn't going to tell them, that as soon as the events were over with for the day, he had every intention of heading to Dallas with the signed divorce papers for the final showdown with his wife. It wasn't something he was looking forward to, but he had put it off long enough. It was time that they both got on with the business of living.

When the cowboy gave him a short nod, indicating that he was ready for his turn at trying to ride the bull, Sam pulled the rope and opened the chute gate. As he watched Black Mamba get rid of the man on his back as if he was little more than a pesky fly, Sam watched Ryder spring into action and divert the bull while the cowboy sprinted to safety.

Normally, he enjoyed watching his brother play chicken with an angry bull. But for reasons Sam couldn't quite put his finger on, Ryder's daredevil antics didn't hold his attention the way they used to. In fact, since returning to work a week ago, he found that being on the road all the time didn't hold nearly the appeal that it once had, either.

Sam frowned. Had his forced downtime changed him that much?

As he thought about staying at home with Bria and what they had shared, he found himself with more regrets than just a few. She was right. In the past, he hadn't taken the time to be with her the way he should have. She was also right about him not having to be on the road if he didn't want to be. The Sugar Creek Rodeo Company was highly successful and one of the main reasons was due to the men he had hired to wrangle the animals. They were all good at their jobs and any one of them could oversee things while they were traveling from one rodeo to another. And usually one of his brothers was either competing in or working the rodeos that had contracted him to supply the livestock. They would be more than happy to keep an eye out for any problems that arose.

He took a deep breath and then another as he came to terms with what Bria had been trying to tell him all along. He had wanted to give her everything she ever wanted. But he had missed seeing that by spending time with her the way he had when he was off work with the concussion, he was doing just that—giving her her heart's desire.

He shook his head at his own foolishness when he realized where his heart really was. It was back at Sugar Creek Ranch. Unfortunately, his reason for wanting to be there—hell, his reason for living—wasn't.

Glancing at his watch, he motioned for his brother, T.J. "Take over for me."

"Where are you going? Are you all right?" T.J. asked, frowning. "I've never known you to leave before a rodeo is over." He shook his head. "At least, when they aren't hauling your butt out on a stretcher."

"I have something I need to take care of," Sam answered, handing him the gate rope.

"Does your business happen to be in Dallas?" T.J. asked, grinning.

He shook his head. "Don't be a smart-ass."

"Tell Bria we all said hey," Ryder called as he positioned himself next to T.J. at the chute gate.

Ignoring his brothers, Sam quickly made his way out of the arena and through the personnel exit to his truck. He had no idea what he was going to say to her or if it would make any difference with her.

All he knew for sure was that he had to try. He would regret every single moment of every single day for the rest of his life if he didn't.

Nine

"Are you sure you're going to be all right?" Mariah asked, looking concerned.

"I'm going to be fine," Bria said. "I just need a little time to come to terms with everything that's happened and get myself back on track."

"Are you sure that's all this is?" Mariah's expression was doubtful. "All you've wanted to do since you returned to Dallas is sleep."

"It's easier to sleep than to think about things." Bria hoped her smile was encouraging. "But you didn't stop by on your way down to Shady Grove to worry over me. Tell me about your new job and your move down there."

Mariah brightened instantly and as she chattered on about her new job as the office manager of a medical clinic in the rural ranching community, Bria allowed her mind to wander. In the two weeks since leaving Sugar

Creek Ranch all she seemed to be able to do was cry and sleep. She had chalked up her uncharacteristic behavior to the emotional upset she had suffered because of Sam's duplicity, but the doctor she had seen just that morning had other ideas to explain her unusual fatigue and unstable emotions. She was pregnant.

How it was possible to already be experiencing some of the early symptoms of pregnancy was still a mystery to her, but the doctor had assured her that it wasn't all that uncommon and the blood test he had run confirmed his diagnosis. Because of the night she had spent making love with Sam, she was going to have a baby— Sam's baby.

But as happy as she was about having their child, she still had a hard time believing he would deceive her the way he had. It was true, he hadn't lied to her. But by failing to tell her that he had regained his memory, he hadn't exactly been truthful with her either.

"Bria, are you listening to me?" Mariah asked, frowning.

"I'm sorry," Bria said, turning her attention back to her sister. "What were you saying?"

Mariah reached across the table to touch Bria's hand. "I asked if you've heard from Sam."

"No. We haven't had any contact since I left the ranch." She took a deep breath in an effort to ease the tightening in her chest. "Nate called to ask how I'm doing and to let me know that the neurologist had given Sam a clean bill of health and released him to go back to work, but that's all I've heard."

"I'm sure he'll be in touch with you soon," Mariah

said, her tone sympathetic. "He's never impressed me as being the kind of man who gives up so easily. Besides, I saw the way he looked at you at Jaron's birthday dinner. There isn't a doubt in my mind that Sam is still head over heels in love with you."

Tears began to well up in Bria's eyes as she shook her head. "There was never any doubt about our love, Mariah. But a marriage is more than two people caring deeply for each other. It's sharing your entire life with that person—the good and the bad." She swiped at her tears with the back of her hand. "Sam has never really done that with me. Maybe if he had, I'd be able to understand why he's so driven and why he puts working ahead of our marriage."

"I'm so sorry, Bria," Mariah said, rising to her feet to come around the table to hug her. "I didn't mean to make you cry."

"It's not your fault." She hugged her younger sister back. "This has been an extremely emotional time for me and it's going to take a while to get my feet back under me again."

Mariah nodded as she returned to her chair. "I understand completely. You've already been through breaking up with Sam once. Now you're having to go through it all over again." She wiped away a tear of her own. "That has to make it doubly hard to get through this now."

"Don't worry," she said, smiling through her tears. "It's going to be tough for a while, but I'll get over it. I have to."

Bria didn't tell her sister that she had no other choice but to survive for the baby's sake. She hadn't told anyone about the pregnancy and even though she was still so very hurt and angry with Sam, she felt he should be the first one to know about the baby.

It saddened her to think that their child would have to be shuttled back and forth between his or her parents, but that couldn't be helped. Sam had made his choice and she had made hers. All there was left to do now was to move forward and make the best of the situation for their child.

"I suppose I should get back on the road," Mariah said, standing up. "I'd really like to get down to Shady Grove and unload the car before it's too dark to see what I'm doing."

"How big is the house you've rented?" Bria asked, following her sister to the door.

"You'll have to come down for a weekend once I get settled in," Mariah said, becoming animated. "It's a cute little two-bedroom cottage just outside of town with a white picket fence around the yard and a swimming pool and hot tub off the back patio."

"It sounds ideal for you." She gave her sister a hug. "Let me know when you're ready for company and I'll drive down for a visit."

"Absolutely," Mariah said, hugging her back. Opening the door, her sister stopped dead in her tracks. "Oh, dear."

"What's wrong?" Bria asked, looking around Mariah to see what had startled her sister.

Bria's heart came to a screeching halt, then took off as if she were running a race at the sight of Sam climbing the steps to her apartment. He was dressed as always in a chambray shirt, well-worn blue jeans, scuffed boots and his wide-brimmed black Resistol, but she didn't think he had ever looked more handsome or sexy.

"Are you going to be okay with him being here?" Mariah whispered. "I can stay if you need me."

"Don't worry," Bria said. "I'll be fine. We need to discuss a few details about the divorce anyway and now is as good a time as any to get that done."

"Hi…Sam," Mariah said, sounding a bit hesitant.

"Mariah." Sam nodded at his sister-in-law, but his eyes never left the woman standing just behind her.

"I, uh, have to go." He watched Mariah turn to glance at Bria.

"You have a safe trip and call or text me when you get to Shady Grove so that I'll know you made it all right," Bria said calmly.

"I will," Mariah assured her. "Good luck, Sam," Mariah mouthed silently as she walked past him to descend the stairs to the apartment-complex parking area.

He smiled and gave the pretty brunette a short nod of understanding, then focused on Bria. She looked good. Damn good. It had been two weeks since she left the ranch and seeing her now was food for his soul.

"I'm sorry I didn't call," he said when he reached the landing and came to stand in front of her. They stared at each other for a moment before he asked, "Is this a good time for you?"

She hadn't moved from the open doorway and he wasn't entirely sure she was going to invite him in. As she stared at him for several more long, agonizing seconds, he thought she was going to refuse, but finally nodding, she stepped back for him to enter the small apartment.

"I do need to talk to you about changing some of the terms in the divorce papers," she said, leading the way to the living room.

Looking around, Sam noticed the pictures that used to hang on the wall by the staircase at the ranch house. They were all there—pictures of his brothers and her family—except their wedding picture. It was conspicuously absent from the collection. He briefly wondered where she had put it, but that was secondary to his main concern. He had to find a way to get her to give him one more chance. And this time he was determined to get it right.

"This seems like a fairly nice place," he said politely. He didn't mean a word of it. It wasn't their ranch house where she belonged.

"It's a little small, but I don't need a lot of room," she said, motioning for him to sit down on the couch.

Sam took a large folded envelope from his hip pocket and lowered himself to the cushions while she settled herself in a chair across the coffee table from him. Neither spoke, and he hated the awkwardness between them.

"Here are the signed papers," he finally said, placing the envelope on the coffee table. "Getting a divorce isn't what I want now any more than I did three and a half months ago." He took a deep breath. "But I love you too much to stand in the way of you being happy, sweetheart." He looked directly into her eyes and hoped she recognized the truth in his words. "I swear, your happiness is all I've ever wanted, Bria."

"But I wasn't happy, Sam." He watched her capture her lower lip between her teeth to keep it from trembling a moment before she added, "You gave me everything you thought I wanted—clothes, the house, jewelry. I appreciated them, but none of those things meant as much to me as being with you. All I ever wanted was *you*, but you were never there with me and I got tired of being alone."

He noticed that she hadn't reached for the papers and hoped that was a good sign. Maybe she wasn't as anxious to be rid of him as he had first thought.

He sat forward and, propping his forearms on his knees, stared down at his loosely clasped hands. "I realize now just how hard it must have been on you with me being gone all the time and I'm sorry for that."

"Yes, it was hard," she agreed. "I wanted my husband to want to be with me more than he wanted to be with his livestock."

Sam knew that now would be the time to explain why he was so driven to succeed, why he felt compelled to work hard to give her everything her heart desired. But it wasn't going to be easy for him. He had left that life behind when the state removed him and Nate from the house their father had abandoned them in some eighteen years ago and he wasn't in the habit of looking back.

He had never been the nervous type, but his entire life seemed to hinge on what he was about to say and it was tying him in knots. "My mother died from a massive stroke when I was twelve and Nate was ten," he said, not quite sure where else to start.

"I'm so sorry, Sam," Bria said, her voice filled with compassion. "That must have been terribly hard for you and Nate."

For the first time in years, Sam allowed himself to think about the hurt and abandonment he had felt when his mother passed. He damn near choked on the emotion and, pushing it to the back of his mind, cleared his throat in order to continue.

"She sometimes worked two jobs to keep a roof over our heads and food in our mouths," he said, hating that he hadn't been old enough to help her.

"Where was…your father?" Bria asked quietly.

Sam clenched his jaw so hard, he was surprised his teeth didn't crumble from the pressure. "The son of a bitch sat flat on his ass and watched her work herself to death."

Her soft gasp seemed to echo throughout the small room, and he wasn't certain if she was shocked at Joe Rafferty's laziness or the anger in his tone. "That's why you work so hard and never took time off unless you were forced to, isn't it?" she asked.

Unable to sit still any longer, Sam nodded and stood up to prowl the room. "I was determined when we got married not to be anything like my father. I wasn't going to sit back and watch my wife struggle to support us like he did with my mother. I wanted to make sure that I could provide the best life possible for you and the family we wanted to have."

She looked confused. "Why didn't you explain this

to me all those times I asked why you were working so hard? Didn't you think I would understand that not wanting to be like your father was what motivated you?" She shook her head. "All you would ever tell me was that you were working to ensure our future and that you wanted me to have nice things."

In hindsight, he realized that it would have saved them both a lot of heartache if he had told her about his childhood up front. But once he had been removed from the situation, it wasn't something that he cared to revisit.

"I guess I figured that if I told you about my situation as a kid, you'd know you married a man that wasn't nearly good enough for you."

"Sam Rafferty, don't ever let me hear you say something like that about yourself again," she said forcefully. "You're a good man. No one works harder or has more ambition than you."

He shrugged. "I think you'd better hold that opinion until I finish telling you what led me and Nate to become wards of the state."

"I can't see that it will change my mind about you, but go ahead," she encouraged. "I'm listening."

"Everything was okay while Mom was alive. We didn't have much, but she somehow managed to provide the necessities. But after she died, more times than not when we came home from school, there wasn't anything in the house to eat and the old man was nowhere to be found." He took a deep breath in order to tell her the rest. "So we started shoplifting food from a little market in the neighborhood."

"You were twelve years old and hungry, Sam," she said gently. "You did what you had to do to survive."

"It still wasn't right." He shook his head. "But that wasn't the worst of it." Running his hand across the back of his neck to ease the building tension, he continued, "We found a gun the old man had stashed away on a closet shelf, and at first we only carried it in case someone tried to stop us from taking the food we needed. We figured all we would have to do is point it at them and they'd let us go. By the time I turned fifteen, the old man had disappeared completely and we had graduated to robbing stores at gunpoint in order to pay the rent and keep from having to sleep in the streets."

"Oh, my God, Sam!" The shocked expression on her pretty face just about tore him apart. It was the look he expected, but it didn't make it any easier for him to see. "Is that why you were sent to Hank Calvert's ranch?"

He nodded. "Nate had tried robbing a convenience store on his own and it didn't go well. He got away, but detectives had been watching us for several weeks and knew we were the ones they were looking for. When they found us, I told them I was the one who pulled the robbery."

"Why?" she asked, frowning.

"Fifteen-year-old boys don't think things through," he said, smiling sardonically. "I got it in my head that if the police thought I had acted alone, they would let Nate go."

"But they knew you were both involved," she guessed.

He nodded. "They had enough evidence from the

previous robberies that had we been of age, they would have locked us up and thrown away the key."

"What kept you out of juvenile detention?" she asked, clearly surprised that they hadn't been sent there to begin with.

"We were assigned a children's advocate who took the time to find out about our mom dying and the old man abandoning us. I don't know whether it was out of pity or if she recognized that we had only been trying to survive, but she worked a miracle." Sam shook his head. "I don't know how she did it, but she made a deal with the D.A. to have us both sent to the Last Chance Ranch and the judge went along with it."

Sam would forever be grateful to the overworked, underpaid civil-service worker. The woman had spared him and Nate from being sent into an environment that might have hardened them beyond redemption, as well as saving them from themselves.

"You might have started down the wrong path, but Hank turned you and Nate around," Bria pointed out.

"Hank helped us realize that the life we were leading wasn't what our mother would have wanted for us."

"What gave you the idea I wouldn't understand about your childhood, Sam?"

"Pride, I guess."

Bria could tell that Sam was ashamed of his past and would just as soon forget that it ever happened. But he had to understand that he was the man he was today because of it.

"You and Nate have both risen above your problems," she said, choosing her words carefully. "No matter what happened when you were younger, you grew up to be honest, hardworking men. Good men."

She watched him take a deep breath. "This isn't easy for me to say, but I guess I've always been afraid I'd revert to the kind of no-good man my father was if I didn't keep my nose to the grindstone."

"Oh, Sam, that's the last thing you would do," she said, shaking her head. "That's not who you are."

Bria wanted to go to him, wanted to wrap her arms around him and erase all the hurt and disillusionment that he had experienced during his youth. But she didn't dare. Although she understood now why he was so driven to succeed, it didn't mean he was willing to abandon being a workaholic.

"There's something else you need to know," he said, walking back over to sit down on the couch.

"What's that?" she asked, wondering what other injustices he might have suffered as a boy.

"The reason I have a hard time accepting that you want to do things for me is because I don't want you to see me any other way but strong and capable," he said hesitantly. "A man who can take care of you, not a weak, useless excuse for a human being."

"Dear God, Sam, why would you think I would see you any other way?" she asked, confused.

"I guess when that's all you heard for as long as you can remember, you start to believe it," he said, shrugging.

She caught her breath as she began to understand. "Your father was…abusive."

When Sam raised his eyes to meet hers, he nodded.

"He wasn't physically abusive, but verbally, he really did a number on me. Most of the time he ignored me and Nate as if we didn't exist. But when he did say something to us, it was never anything positive. If we heard how worthless and pathetic we were once, we heard it a thousand times—usually when we were taking our mother's attention away from him."

Anger filled Bria at the thought of anyone talking that way to a child. But for his father to have spoken that way to Sam was almost more than she could bear.

"Your father was the one who was weak, Sam. He tried to build himself up by bringing you down."

"I know that now," he said, smiling sadly. "But having it drilled into you from the time you're old enough to listen has a lasting effect." He seemed to take an inordinate interest in his boots a moment before he lifted his gaze to meet hers. "That's why I failed you when you needed me the most, sweetheart."

Bria sucked in a sharp breath. "You mean when I lost the baby."

For the first time since she had known him, he allowed her to see the deep sadness and emotional pain in the depths of his dark blue eyes. "I didn't come home right away because I couldn't," he said. "I couldn't let you see how much your losing the baby affected me."

Tears filled her eyes. "But I needed you, Sam. I needed you to share the grief and disappointment I was going through—that we were both going through."

He closed his eyes and the sight of a lone tear slowly making its way down his lean cheek almost tore her heart out. Sam had been just as hurt by the miscarriage as she had been, but because he feared that he would appear weak, he had chosen to bottle up his emotions and act as if nothing had happened.

Before she could get out of the chair and go to him, he cleared his throat, got to his feet and started toward the door. "I'm sorry I failed you, Bria. Whatever else you want in the divorce, just have the lawyer draw up the necessary papers and I'll sign them."

"No."

Stopping, he turned to face her. She had never seen him look more miserable.

"What does that mean?" he asked, his voice rough.

Bria rose from the chair and walked over to stand in front of him. "No, you didn't fail me, Sam."

"How the hell do you figure that?" he asked, frowning. "I wasn't around when you lost the baby and I was too big of a coward to come home to face the emotions we were both going through."

She placed her hand on his arm. "Sam, I think we failed each other."

"Don't say that, sweetheart." He shook his head. "I couldn't have asked for a better wife."

"Yes, you could." She swiped at the tears running down her cheeks. "I knew you had problems when you were younger and should have realized that you had to build a lot of walls to protect yourself. And instead of whining about you never being home with me, I should have understood when you said you worked so hard because you were trying to be a good husband."

"That's no excuse for me not sharing my past with you, for me not being with you when you lost the baby," he said stubbornly. "I'll never forgive myself for being such a damn coward."

"Oh, Sam, just shut up and hold me," she said, wrapping her arms around his waist and laying her head against his wide chest. Maybe if she could convince him that she forgave him, one day he would be able to forgive himself.

When he didn't immediately take her into his arms, she leaned back to look up at him. "Sam?"

"I can't put my arms around you, Bria."

"Why not?"

"Because if I do, I'll never be able—" he stopped to clear his throat and she knew he was once again fighting a wave of strong emotion "—to let you go."

Bria knew they had reached a crossroad. She could either continue with the divorce and be miserable without the man she loved for the rest of her life or accept things for the way they were and live with the man who had stolen her heart the moment they met.

"I don't want you to ever let me go," she said, knowing in her soul that she had chosen the right path. "I want you to hold me forever, Sam."

He immediately wrapped his arms around her and crushed her to him. "I don't deserve you, Bria. But I give you my word that every single minute of every day for the rest of my life, I'll do my damnedest to prove to you how much I love you and how grateful I am that you're my wife."

When he lowered his head to capture her lips with his, Bria's heart soared. There was so much love and emotion in his kiss that it left her breathless.

"I have something I need to tell you," she said when he finally broke the kiss.

"You can tell me anything, sweetheart." He kissed her forehead. "You know everything about me now and I give you my word, there won't be any more secrets between us."

"I have a secret that I need to confess," she said, glancing up at him. "It appears that you got your wish."

Bewilderment crossed his handsome face. "Would you like to clarify that?"

"Before I left the ranch that morning, you said that you might have made me pregnant," she said, smiling. "You got your wish."

His confused expression quickly turned into a wide grin. "Really?"

She nodded. "I went to the doctor this morning because I wasn't feeling quite right."

"Are you okay? There isn't a problem, is there?" His concern was endearing.

"No problems," she assured him. "I'm just sleepy all the time and my emotions are a little unpredictable."

"But you're okay?"

"I'm wonderful," she said, kissing his chin. "I'm going to have a baby. Our baby."

She let out a startled squeak when he swung her up in his arms and carried her over to sit down on the couch. Settling her on his lap, he held her close.

"This is a new beginning for us, Bria. A second chance." He gave her a smile that sent a shiver of anticipation straight up her spine. "I think we should do something to mark the occasion."

"What did you have in mind?" she asked, loving him more with each passing second.

"I think we should do that vow-renewal thing," he said, looking thoughtful. "Then we can throw a big party and let everyone help us celebrate."

"I love that idea," she agreed. "But we'll have to start making plans well in advance in order for you to take the time off from being on the road with the rodeo company."

"We won't have to worry about that." The love in his blue gaze caused a spark of hope to ignite in her chest. "I did a lot of soul-searching this past couple of weeks and found that being gone all the time isn't what I want any more than you do. I'm coming off the road and going to manage everything from the ranch." He smiled. "I'll be around so much, you'll probably start complaining about me being underfoot all the time."

"Never. Oh, Sam, I love you so much," she said, throwing her arms around his neck.

"And I love you, sweetheart." He kissed her until they both gasped for air. "Now let's get down to planning this shindig. I want to make you mine."

"I'm already yours," she promised. "And you're mine."

"For the rest of our lives," he said.

Epilogue

Sam stood with his brothers, watching Bria and some of their other guests at the vow-renewal party form a line as the band struck up a Brooks and Dunn tune about boot scootin'. He loved watching her dance, loved to watch her body move in time to the music. Hell, he just plain loved everything about her.

"Sam, I swear you've been wearing that same sappy grin for the past few months," T.J. said, taking a swig from the beer bottle in his hand.

"Yeah, the way you're acting, anyone would think you had just drawn an inside straight," Lane added, laughing.

"I can't help it," Sam said, shrugging. He winked at Bria. "I'm a happy man these days."

"You don't miss being out on the road?" Jaron asked, sounding skeptical.

"Nope. I've got everything I want right here at home," Sam assured him.

When the song ended, Bria and Mariah walked over to join the group. "Do you think we should tell everyone our news, sweetheart?" he whispered, putting his arm around her shoulders and drawing her to his side.

They had agreed to wait until Bria was past the first trimester in her pregnancy to tell anyone about the baby, and Sam was itching to let his brothers know that he was going to be a daddy.

"Go right ahead," she said, smiling up at him.

"Do y'all think you're up to babysitting in about six months?" Sam asked, giving them a meaningful look.

"Hot damn!" Nate exclaimed, grinning from ear to ear. "I'm going to be an uncle."

"Congratulations," Ryder said, hugging Bria. "But you do realize you'll have two kids to tend to when the baby is born, instead of just this big lug, don't you?"

Sam didn't think he had ever seen her look more radiant when she said, "If I have any problems with Sam or the baby, I'll let you know, Ryder."

"No wonder you've been so damn smug." Grinning, Lane slapped Sam on the back. "You've been working on a full house."

"I reserve the right to spoil my nephew," Jaron announced.

"My niece is going to be a little princess," Mariah said, shaking her head.

"Nope, it's going to be a boy," Jaron insisted. "I'm sure of it."

Mariah glared at him. "You couldn't be more wrong,

Mr. Lambert. Besides, you don't know diddly-squat about pregnancy and babies."

As Mariah and Jaron continued to argue over the baby's sex, T.J. added his congratulations. "Boy or girl, I'm betting we all turn out to be absolute fools over him or her."

"So who's going to be next to jump into the pool of the blissfully hitched?" Sam asked.

"Don't look at me," Nate said, shaking his head. "I'm having too much fun playing the field."

"Well, it isn't going to be me," Lane announced. "I don't have time for a woman in my life right now." He looked at T.J. "Is that neighbor lady still letting her stud jump the fence?"

T.J.'s face turned beet red. "Yes, but don't think I'm looking to hook up with the likes of her. I'd rather run naked through a briar patch."

They all looked at Jaron still arguing with Mariah, shook their heads, then turned their attention to Ryder.

"Oh, no. Don't think I'm looking to take a dip in that pool," Ryder said, shaking his head.

"You're the only one of us who brought a date this evening," Nate pointed out.

Ryder looked fit to be tied. "She's not a date."

Lane cocked one dark eyebrow. "And if you believe that, boys, I've got some prime real estate in Death Valley I'd like to sell you."

"Summer is just a friend," Ryder insisted.

"Then you won't mind if I ask her out?" Nate asked.

"She won't go," Ryder retorted.

"This could go on awhile," Sam said, grinning at

Bria. "Would you like me to bribe the band to play a slow tune so I can hold you?"

"That sounds good to me," she said as they turned toward the dance floor.

As they began moving in time to a slow, romantic song, Sam gazed down at Bria. She was his world, his reason for living and he thanked the good Lord above that she knew all his faults and loved him anyway.

"I love you, Mrs. Rafferty."

"And I love you, Mr. Rafferty," she said. "For the rest of our lives."

* * * * *

#2167 A SCANDAL SO SWEET
Ann Major

When a billionaire entrepreneur and an actress with a scandalous past are reunited, they quickly find that the fire of their passion has never died.

#2168 GILDED SECRETS
The Highest Bidder
Maureen Child

Can he seduce the single mother's secrets out of her before they bring the world's most glamorous auction house to its knees?

#2169 STRICTLY TEMPORARY
Billionaires and Babies
Robyn Grady

Stranded in a snowstorm with an abandoned baby, two strangers create their own heat in each other's arms.

#2170 THE CINDERELLA ACT
The Drummond Vow
Jennifer Lewis

A hedge-fund billionaire falls for his housekeeper, but will duty to his pregnant ex-wife and class differences keep them from finding true love?

#2171 A MAN OF PRIVILEGE
Sarah M. Anderson

When a blue-blooded lawyer falls for his impoverished witness, it's a conflict of interest and a clash of different worlds.

#2172 MORE THAN HE EXPECTED
Andrea Laurence

A no-strings fling? That's what this avowed bachelor thought he wanted...until he finds his past lover pregnant—and sexier than ever!

REQUEST YOUR FREE BOOKS!
2 FREE NOVELS PLUS 2 FREE GIFTS!

Harlequin *Desire*

ALWAYS POWERFUL, PASSIONATE AND PROVOCATIVE

YES! Please send me 2 FREE Harlequin Desire® novels and my 2 FREE gifts (gifts are worth about $10). After receiving them, if I don't wish to receive any more books, I can return the shipping statement marked "cancel." If I don't cancel, I will receive 6 brand-new novels every month and be billed just $4.30 per book in the U.S. or $4.99 per book in Canada. That's a saving of at least 14% off the cover price! It's quite a bargain! Shipping and handling is just 50¢ per book in the U.S. and 75¢ per book in Canada.* I understand that accepting the 2 free books and gifts places me under no obligation to buy anything. I can always return a shipment and cancel at any time. Even if I never buy another book, the two free books and gifts are mine to keep forever.

225/326 HDN FEF3

Name _____ (PLEASE PRINT)

Address _____ Apt. #

City _____ State/Prov. _____ Zip/Postal Code

Signature (if under 18, a parent or guardian must sign)

Mail to the **Reader Service:**
IN U.S.A.: P.O. Box 1867, Buffalo, NY 14240-1867
IN CANADA: P.O. Box 609, Fort Erie, Ontario L2A 5X3

Not valid for current subscribers to Harlequin Desire books.

Want to try two free books from another line?
Call 1-800-873-8635 or visit www.ReaderService.com.

* Terms and prices subject to change without notice. Prices do not include applicable taxes. Sales tax applicable in N.Y. Canadian residents will be charged applicable taxes. Offer not valid in Quebec. This offer is limited to one order per household. All orders subject to credit approval. Credit or debit balances in a customer's account(s) may be offset by any other outstanding balance owed by or to the customer. Please allow 4 to 6 weeks for delivery. Offer available while quantities last.

Your Privacy—The Reader Service is committed to protecting your privacy. Our Privacy Policy is available online at www.ReaderService.com or upon request from the Reader Service.

We make a portion of our mailing list available to reputable third parties that offer products we believe may interest you. If you prefer that we not exchange your name with third parties, or if you wish to clarify or modify your communication preferences, please visit us at www.ReaderService.com/consumerschoice or write to us at Reader Service Preference Service, P.O. Box 9062, Buffalo, NY 14269. Include your complete name and address.

HDES11B

New York Times *and* USA TODAY *bestselling author Vicki Lewis Thompson returns with yet another irresistible cowpoke! Meet Mathew Tredway—cowboy, horse whisperer and honorary Son of Chance.*

Read on for a sneak peek from the bestselling miniseries
SONS OF CHANCE:

LEAD ME HOME
Available July 2012 only from Harlequin® Blaze™.

AS MATTHEW RETURNED to the corral and Houdini, the taste of Aurelia's mouth was on his lips and her scent clung to his clothes. He'd briefly satisfied the craving growing within him, and like a light snack before a meal, it would have to do.

When he'd first walked into the kitchen, his mind had been occupied with the challenge of training Houdini. He'd thought his concentration would hold long enough to get some carrots, ask about the corn bread and leave before succumbing to Aurelia's appeal. He'd miscalculated. Within a very short time, desire had claimed every brain cell.

Although seducing her this morning was out of the question, his libido had demanded some sort of satisfaction. He'd tried to deny that urge and had nearly made it out of the house. Apparently his willpower was no match for the temptation of Aurelia's mouth, though, and he'd turned around.

If he'd ever felt this kind of desperate need for a woman, he couldn't recall it. During the night, as he'd lain in his narrow bunk listening to the cowhands snore, he'd searched for an explanation as to why Aurelia affected him this way.

Sometime in the early-morning hours he'd come up with

the answer. After years of dating women who were rolling stones like he was, he'd developed an itch for a hearth-and-home kind of woman. Aurelia, with her cooking skills and voluptuous body, could give him that.

With luck, once he'd scratched this particular itch, he'd be fine again. He certainly hoped so, because he had no intention of giving up his career, and travel was a built-in requirement. Plus he liked to travel and had no real desire to stay in one spot and become domesticated.

Tonight he'd say all that to Aurelia, because he didn't want her going into this with any illusions about perma-nence. He figured that when the right guy came along, she'd get married and have kids.

Too bad that guy wouldn't be him....

Will Aurelia be the one to corral this cowboy for good?
Find out in: LEAD ME HOME

Available July 2012
wherever Harlequin® Blaze™ books are sold.

This summer, celebrate everything Western
with Harlequin® Books!

www.Harlequin.com/Western

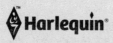

Debut author

Kathy Altman

takes you on a moving journey
of forgiveness and second chances.

One year after losing her husband in Afghanistan,
Parker Dean finds Corporal Reid Macfarland at her
door with a heartfelt confession and a promise to save
her family business. Although Reid is the last person
Parker should trust her livelihood to, she finds herself
captivated by his silent courage. Together,
can they learn to forgive and love again?

The Other Soldier

Available July 2012 wherever books are sold.

This summer, celebrate everything Western
with Harlequin® Books!

www.Harlequin.com/Western

HSR71790